# THE
# SCATTERING
of the HEATHER

# THE
# SCATTERING
## of the HEATHER

*Stories of the Sinclairs and Kin on Six Continents*

*To Richard Sonia*

*With affection.*

*John*

10/11/2010

**John Henderson Sinclair**

Manufactured in the United States of America

10 9 8 7 6 5 4 3 2 1

∞ The paper used in this publication meets the minimum requirements of the American National Standard for Information Sciences—Permanence for Printed Library Materials, ANSI Z39.48–1984.

The page vi epigraph is from Sir Walter Scott's "Love of Country."

International Standard Book Number
ISBN 13: 978-0-615-38375-0 (paper)

*To my beloved wife, Maxine, and our sons, David, Paul, and John Mark*

The John H. Sinclair family at John O'Groats, 1969

(eldest son, David, was in the Czech Republic at the time)

*Breathes there a man with soul so dead*
*Who never to himself hath said,*
*"This is my own, my native land!"*
*Whose heart hath ne'er within him burned*
*As home his footsteps he hath turned,*
*From wandering on a foreign strand?*
*If such there breathes, go, mark him well!*
*For him no minstrel raptures swell.*

# Contents

*Photo section follows p. 86*

# Preface

*The Scattering of the Heather* narrates stories of the Sinclairs of Caithness who put down roots on far-flung frontiers in six continents over the past two centuries. I do not seek to imitate the masterful epic *Blood and Kin: An Empire Saga,* written by Andrew Sinclair. That work stands on its own merits. Rather, I am attempting to tell stories of near and distant relatives who since 1795 have scattered, like the heather, across the world and left their imprint on other pages of history. These persons were not outstanding members of society but women and men whose lives were mostly lived with dignity and honor, but lived in obscurity.

The stories in this book are based on the lives of my ancestors, but I have fictionalized some of them, even changing names. Where the facts were missing in these stories, imagination has filled in the gaps. Few of the characters can be called empire builders, but they have left their footprints as social, intellectual, and religious activists and have spread the seed of Scottish culture and values wherever it has found hospitable climate and soil.

Over the past two decades, I have traveled far and wide to Australia, New Zealand, South Africa, the People's Republic of China, Chile, Venezuela, Colombia, Great Britain, and North America to research the lives of the scattered Sinclairs and their relatives. I invite the reader to, likewise, "sail across the ocean waters of history, trawl and land a catch for their delight and edification."[1]

This book is published in the year following the 250th anniversary of the birth of Robert Burns, the Ploughman Poet, whose words captured the spirit of the Scottish people. That commemorative year was declared Scotland's Homecoming Year, in which Scots all over the world were encouraged to visit the homeland. An estimated thirty million people around the world claim Scottish descent, representing about one-half of one percent of the world's population. This figure does not include millions more non-Scottish families with relatives who came from Scotland.

Since few of these millions were able to make the pilgrimage to Scotland, I offer in these pages glimpses of lives lived out on six continents. I assume the role of the *seannachie,* bards among the Highlander clans who traditionally recited the royal lineages and preserved clan traditions. That sacred mantle fell into disuse long ago, but today it is played out on the Internet, genealogical societies, church archives, courthouses, and universities, and by some intrepid authors.

When heather dies, it becomes a part of the earth from which it sprung—a part of the duff. The heather becomes, in its decay, peat, a source of light and warmth burning in the hearth of both cottage and castle. In its demise, it greatly increases in value. The Sinclairs, like peat, leave a life-giving glow after they wither and die. Some of their lives may even become a kind of spiritual peat, contributing to the renewal of the human race.

I am indebted to my wife, Maxine Banta Sinclair, for her careful reading of the manuscript and insightful suggestions. Our three sons, David, Paul, and John Mark, have also encouraged their father in this literary adventure, as have other friends who have read portions of the text. Most of my relatives referred to in these stories are no longer living. However, my sister Clare ("Margaret") and our son John Mark, his wife, Marcela, and their children, Gabriel Raul and Natalia Alondra, have given me permission to write about them. To all, I am grateful for their inspiration, assistance, and practical suggestions. My gratitude goes, as well, to my editor, Michael Hanson, for his skill and advice in the preparation of this book.

John Henderson Sinclair
July 2010

# Foreword

*Looking in the Mirror of History: A Perspective*

We are nothing without our roots because "that which is born in the bone can never be driven out of the blood." John Henderson Sinclair's book, *The Scattering of the Heather,* describes how Scottish people can be found on every continent, resulting from centuries of emigration—both voluntary and otherwise. No single period in Scotland's long history played a greater role in creating that diaspora than the Highland Clearances. Over 150 years, that part of Scotland was dramatically shaped by the social and political changes that followed the battle of Culloden in 1746—a battle that the Sinclairs skillfully managed to avoid (even as one of the English regiments was commanded by a Sinclair!).

The battle wasn't specifically the English v. the Scots, because the Hanoverian army of 9,000 men comprised several companies of Argyll militia and Highlanders raised from the Protestant Clan Campbell. There were probably as many Scots fighting for the Hanoverian side as for the Jacobean. Culloden marked the final defeat of the Gallic people, the ancient Celt folk whose clan structure was brutally obliterated as they where banished from the land during the Highland Clearances. Culloden was infamous for the atrocities committed by the victorious Hanoverian army. The city of Inverness was decimated. A way of life was changed forever in the Highlands.

Following the failure of the Jacobite rebellion, the British government extended its control into the mountainous regions of the north, building roads, confiscating land, and prohibiting the traditional powers of the clan chiefs, the wearing of the "Highland dress," and the playing of the bagpipes. The Highlands then experienced a dramatic transition when many of the chiefs, who had become anglicized, assumed the role of landlords. They sold their estates to the newly enriched industrialists, who had little concern for the crofters (owners or tenants of a small farm).

In addition there had been a massive population boom, and there was only minimal work through marginal agriculture. The Highland Clearances remains one of the darkest chapters in Scottish history. Families who had lived on a small piece of Mother Earth, often little more than an acre, were frequently evicted in the cruelest manner. They tried to defend their homes, but even these were sometimes burned down by brutal bailiffs who were employed solely for that purpose. Sheep were considered to be more profitable than people. The traditional clan ethos, where the clan chief was deemed to be the first among equals, gave way to an antagonistic relationship between landlord and tenant. As far as the landlords were concerned, the crofters were squatters and had to be evicted. Where were they to go? Some turned to fishing, and others were put on ships and deported in a manner that was comparable to the slave trade.

Still others were mercenaries. Scots were to be found in every European army. In France they became the garde du roi, the king's guard. King Gustavus Adolphus of Sweden depended on Scottish mercenaries to control his kingdom. As late as World War I, the Russian arsenal was under the control of Robert Bavre de Saint-Clair, while his elder brother, Nicolas, was an officer in the Life Guards of the Tsarina. That particular Sinclair family fled to Brazil following the Russian Revolution.

The subsequent spread of Scots immigrants brought the Old World and the New World together. Although Scotland has fewer than 5 million inhabitants, an estimated 40 million people around the world claim Scottish ancestry. These include nearly 10 million in the United States, 4.7 million in Canada, 1.5 million in Australia, 130,000 in New Zealand, 800,000 in England, 100,000 in Argentina, and 80,000 in Chile. The departure of people from Scotland may have left that country poorer, but the Americas, in particular, benefited enormously. It was such people who tamed the prairies. It was such immigrants whose descendents eventually helped build the largest industrial nation in the world.

The Scot, it would seem, is never more at home than when abroad. The Scots themselves were emigrants from Ireland who came and mixed with the more numerous Picts and Celts. The Scots are a hybrid people. If there is a difference between the Scot and the English, it is difference without a distinction. However, to tell a Scot that he is no different from an Englishman is to take your life in your own hands. Yet DNA research shows us that those who live north and south of the Scottish–English border are genetically the same.

That is a great sadness because, in truth, we fought each other for over three hundred years because someone drew a line on a map. The battle of Bannockburn (1314), about which the Scots are so proud, like the battle of Culloden, had little to do with Scots v. English, because at that time Scotland and England were no more than Norman colonies.

The commanders on the English side were the de Bohuns and the de Clares, whereas the commanders on the Scottish side were Robert the Bruce, who was born in Essex, and William St. Clair. Robert the Bruce had more land in England than he held in Scotland. He actually swore allegiance to Edward I of England on two occasions. He changed sides no fewer than five times. He is now Scotland's greatest hero. Such is propaganda and the need to have heroes!

John Henderson Sinclair is modest and honest enough to suggest that few of his kinsmen mentioned in *The Scattering of the Heather* can claim to be empire builders. My interpretation is somewhat different. They have shown themselves to be the salt of the earth—even if some have failed along the way. It is the common soldier who wins the wars. So it is the common man who makes up the society, of which the family is the foundation. John's book—about his family—could be the story of many of the 40 million Scots who now reside around the world. They still refer to Scotland as their homeland, however—a homeland that few are ever likely to see. No matter, they have a determination to survive and succeed, yet at the same time to give absolute loyalty to the country of their adoption.

As I read this book, I came to realize that his part of the Sinclair family has indeed been blessed to have him as their bard. In his long career as a missionary, human rights activist, and church leader, he has demonstrated moral courage and brought honor to the Sinclair family name. Let's take a leaf out of John's book and build up our own family tree. As John found, it can take us on an exciting tour of the world that might teach us that, whatever our race, we are all at one with each other in our basic human needs. Our neighbors are not foreigners. They too are our kin.

I commend to readers *The Scattering of the Heather* because it demonstrates how we Scots can make ourselves at home anywhere on the planet and live in peace with people of every race, color, and creed. And knowing how fractious the Scots can be, that simply means that everyone can live in peace if they are prepared to discard the baggage of the past and forgive the trespasses of others. That is today's challenge and today's opportunity.

Niven Sinclair
Noted family historian and benefactor

# THE
# SCATTERING
## of the HEATHER

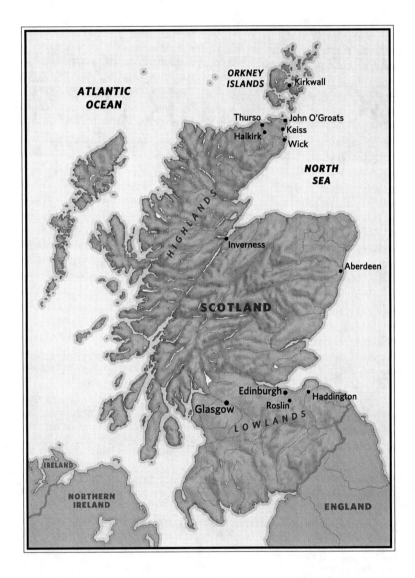

A map of Scotland with locations mentioned in the text

# Prologue

*The Scottish Highlands in the Eighteenth Century*

## The Land

A celebrated traveler visited Caithness in 1769 and recorded the following observation:

> At that time in Caithness, there was not a single cart road, properly so called in the county. . . . The common people are kept in great servitude and most of their time is given to the lairds. . . . They till, dung, sow and harrow a part of the extensive farm of the proprietor . . . the condition of the slaves in the West Indies was infinitely preferable to theirs.[1]

Caithness is the most northern county on the mainland of Scotland. The name is of Scandinavian origin. In Old Norse the county was called "Katanes," which in English means "the nose of Cattey." This description corresponds to the shape of the land, which protrudes to the northeast.

The greater part of the bedrock of Caithness consists of flagstone. The headlands are of sandstone, except the Ord, which is a mass of granite. The county measures 712 square miles and is very flat. There is an almost total absence of trees. The only species that survives is the sycamore, which is able to withstand the northern blasts. The earth floor of the moor is peat moss and decaying vegetable matter.

But nature has supplied the land with plants and flowers. The area offers a highly interesting field for botanists, with more than 420 flowering plants and ferns. White and red clovers are indigenous. There is the Scotch primrose, the bluebell, the foxglove, and the beautiful white gem called grass of Parnassus. The moors and hillsides are covered with the finest heather.

## The People

The clans suffered a resounding defeat by the English in the battle of Culloden in 1746. The rural economy was crumbling, and the crofters were forced off the land by the modernization of agriculture. England demanded more foodstuffs and coveted the potential commercial wealth of the land from grazing sheep and cattle.

The clan chieftains had always honored the principle of *dutchas,* by which they were recognized as the protectors of the crofters, farmers who had no formal land titles. When the land was sold to developers, the poor were left without legal protection. As the crofters were cleared from the land, the independent artisans and small business owners found themselves without customers.

The economic decline of rural Scotland was tragic. In many ways Scotland was changed forever after Culloden. Rural poverty forced the crofters to settle in the coastal villages or immigrate to the far-flung frontiers of the British Empire. The traditional clan system was in shambles.

The Sinclair family is descended from the Saint-Clairs of Normandy, a Viking people who arrived in northwestern France about AD 800. The Saint-Clairs then came over to England with William the Conqueror and the Norman invaders who fought at the Battle of Hastings in 1066. William "the Seemly" Sinclair, two years later, came accompanying the Saxon princess Margaret, who was married to Malcolm III of Canmore. The royal couple was given lands in Rosslyn, Midlothian, in *life rent* (renewable use). Later, these lands were given over to their son in *free heritage* (perpetual possesion). From these first St. Clairs in Rosslyn have descended many Scottish families.

The other major branch of the Sinclairs is known as the Sinclairs of the Isles. Sir Henry St. Clair was created the Earl of Orkney in 1379, then a Norwegian possession. His father, William, married Isabella, Countess of Orkney, and adopted the "Sinclair" spelling. These Sinclairs quickly established themselves as a principal family in Northern Scotland and the Western Isles. The clan was exceedingly difficult and warlike and functioned as a law unto themselves. There was much internecine fighting and wars with the Gunns, Murrays, and Sutherlands. The Sinclairs in this book were mostly descendents from the Sinclairs of the Isles.

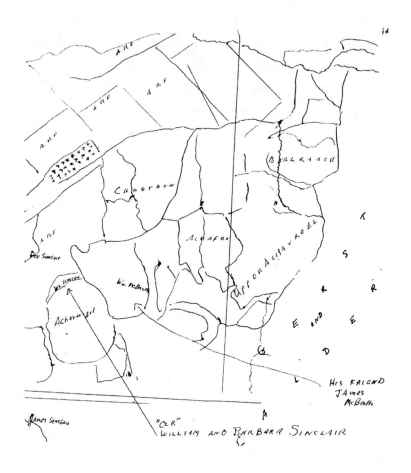

A copy of the ordinance map (1803) with the location
"Achavarigil"

# Finding the Old Land Map

Without the good fortune of finding an old land map, this book could never have been written. I am indebted to my cousin William Clayton Sinclair for its discovery. "Clay" was an investigative reporter for the *Financial Times* of Toronto, Canada. He never left a stone unturned in his profession as a respected journalist and family genealogist.

In the early 1980s, he set out with his wife, Marcelle, to track the earliest records of our Sinclair heritage in County Caithness, Scotland. They found the marriage record of our great-great-grandparents William and Barbara Sinclair in the Church of Scotland parish records. They were married in Halkirk Parish in 1795. A birth record of one of their first children confirmed that William and Barbara lived in the Calder neighborhood, a few miles west of Halkirk.

Clay and Marcelle drove around the area and inquired among the local farmers. They had the good fortune to meet a farmer, named Polson, along a country road and asked him about the history of the area. Clay told him that a Sinclair ancestor had lived there around the 1790s whose name was William Sinclair.

Polson's face lighted up, and he said, "I think I may be able to help you. I have an old map at the farm that is dated 1803. Let's take a look."

At the farm house, Mr. Polson displayed a map with the names and locations of the property owners or tenants. And there was the name, "W. Sinclair—1.2 acres." The next plot over

read, "D. Macbeath—1.6 acres." Macbeath had signed as a witness to the births of William and Barbara's children. Across this
section of the map was printed the traditional Gaelic name of
the property, "Achavarigil."

Mr. Polson said that his brother had purchased the property a few years ago and with it an old stone croft house that
the previous owners said had been there as long as anyone
could remember. Could this building have been the original
croft house where William and Barbara started their married
life in 1795? The telephone company had evidently known the
traditional name of the property since they had posted on the
utility pole at the entrance of the lane the name "Achavarigil."

# 1 | Before the Heather Was Scattered

William Sinclair met Barbara Harrow in 1794 in the village of Halkirk, near the port town of Skarferry. Barbara was in her early twenties, recently widowed with two small children. William, aged thirty-one, was also widowed with four children from his first marriage. William's first wife, Betsy McKay, had been taken quickly by the plague that had swept the country the previous year.

They met after a kirk service in Halkirk, a market town for the farmers living to the west of Wick. The town was surrounded by the most fertile agricultural area in the county. Widow Harrow, just twenty-three, with a small boy tugging at her skirt and a baby girl in her arms, lingered behind in the shade of an old oak tree. Attractive in her Sunday best, she always looked forward to the friendly support in conversation that she received from the church folk. Barbara and her little brood were living with an uncle after her husband's death.

William was a joiner by trade, a craftsman who made wooden plows, carts, and other farm implements. He lived on a small tract three miles west of Halkirk in the Calder neighborhood on property owned by Sir John Sinclair. The area was known by its Gaelic name, "Achavarigil." There, he plied his trade and cared for the four children: Andrew, not yet ten; his younger brother, Donald; and two little sisters.

William Macbeath, his next door neighbor, introduced William and Barbara. He was a blacksmith and worked with William. He made the iron parts for the farm implements that

William fashioned. Macbeath had known Barbara's father when he worked on a fishing boat out of Skarferry.

"William, step over here and meet Barbara, the daughter of an old friend, Captain Harrow," invited Macbeath.

William joined the two and said, "Barbara, it is good to see you after so many years. I remember your father well, and everyone around Skarferry knew him. I am sorry you have been left in sorrow to raise these lovely wee bairns."

"Thank you, kind sir. In some way God will see me through this dark valley," answered Barbara.

On a Sunday afternoon soon afterward, William called on Barbara at her uncle's cottage in Halkirk. The two recently widowed young adults seemed made for each other. Not only did love spring up between them as they got better acquainted, but they soon realized that together they could form a melded family of six children, ages six months through ten years. William had rented a simple stone croft house, no larger than ten feet by twenty, but with space to put in a small loft to sleep the older children and a trundle bed under their parents' bed for the wee ones. They could grow potatoes and barley on the three acres around their dwelling to keep the family alive. Then, too, William was strong and able to earn enough money from his trade to buy the salt, sugar, tea, and other items for a simple country fare.

Love and the need of home did not delay long in forging a brighter future for the new family. By the next spring they had asked the church clerk to post the marriage bans on the kirk door, announcing a late-spring wedding on May 25:

Hereby let it be known that William Sinclair and Barbara Harrow of this parish have declared their intentions to be married. If there is any reason why they may not be joined in Holy Matrimony, let that reason be stated before the elders of this kirk.

Charles McKay, Clerk

Amid the joy of a happy second marriage for William and Barbara, there was discouraging news as small farms were suddenly being bought up by English and lowland Scots in order to turn the plots into pasture for sheep and cattle. Other properties were simply foreclosed by the landlord since it was more profitable not to renew the annual lease that forever had been automatically extended year by year.

The talk at the local store in Halkirk was that the attitudes of the landlords had shifted from a caring paternalism to one of crass entrepreneurship. The local artisans like Sinclair and Macbeath depended on their neighbors for the purchase of the plows and scythes they made. They knew that, even though they had small plots of arable land, they could never support their families without the income from the forge and the carpenter's bench.

One night, after the children were bedded down and asleep, William and Barbara discussed their troubles.

"It looks like the McKays, the Sutherlands, the Hendersons, and the Moodies will be cleared off their lands by the sheriff," William informed Barbara. "Apparently, they now need documents to prove that their leases will be automatically renewed, documents that have never existed."

"But then there will be only six families left: the Bells, Gunns, Nicolsons, Cruikshanks, MacIntires, and Mackays," whispered Barbara. "They have been our best customers and have always paid in cash. How can we survive with only six families as our customers?"

"Perhaps we'll have to move the family to my sister-in-law's rented house down in Wick. I'll try to find work on the harbor construction," offered William. "Since you are expecting our child in three more months, we don't have much time left before we'll be out of meal, sugar, and tea. I'll take the cart and pony tomorrow to Wick and see if the rented house is vacant and if I can find some work on the harbor. I know that if we stay here any longer, it will be too late to make the move and find a place to start all over again. But remember, dear Barbara, the Sinclair clan motto, 'Commit thy work to God.' I don't know how God will take care of us, but all we have left is to trust that God will never let us down."

It was a sad day when, in early September 1805, the Sinclair family started the twenty-mile trek from Halkirk to Wick. William led the pony and cart loaded with the family's meager belongings. Each child carried a small carpet bag and a flask of water for the six-hour walk. The eldest son, Andrew, led the young heifer calf, and Donald, his younger brother, prodded the family pig along.

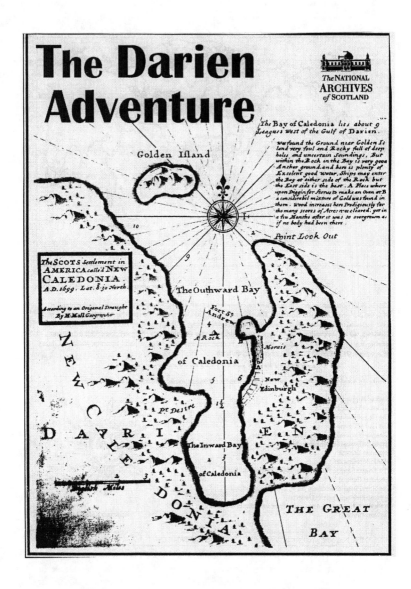

A map of the bay briefly colonized by the Scots (1699), near the border of present-day Panama and Colombia. Reproduced by permission of the Trustees of the National Library of Scotland.

## 2 | The Stobo–Park Family and the Darien Adventure

### The Darien Adventure

Scotland at the end of the seventeenth century was in a state of crisis. Decades of warfare had combined with seven years of famine to drive people from their homes and choke the cities with refugees, some starving to death in the streets. The nation's trade had been crippled by the continual wars of England against continental European powers. Its homegrown industries were withering on the vine. Something had to be done to revive Scotland's economic fortunes before the nation was swallowed up by its richer neighbor to the south.

Financial adventurer William Patterson, a Scot who had made a name for himself as one of the directors of the Bank of England, came up with an audacious scheme to turn Scotland into the major broker for trade between the Pacific and Atlantic oceans. The plan called for the establishment of a trading colony located in a sheltered bay surrounded by friendly Indians and land gifted with rich, fertile soil. The place chosen was the Darien Peninsula near the border of present-day Panama and Colombia. Ships would unload their cargo in a Pacific port, and the goods would be transported overland about forty miles to the Atlantic port of Darien. Scotland would then supplant Holland as the great power broker of the wealth from the East Indies since access to the lucrative Pacific markets would then be made more reliable.

Above all, ships would not have to make the hazardous voyage around Cape Horn at the tip of South America. The planners did not, however, take seriously the challenge that would come from Spain, which claimed control of that region. The entrepreneurs reasoned that they could never make a profit without stepping on someone's toes. Such was the promotional talk to recruit carpenters, masons, soldiers, and sailors for the Darien adventure.

The Company of Scotland was authorized by an act of the Scottish parliament on June 16, 1695, and subscription bonds were opened in Edinburgh in 1696. Soon, the entire capital stock of 400,000 pounds was pledged, and vessels were ordered to be built in Hamburg and Amsterdam. Supplies were purchased, and volunteers were recruited for the expedition. It was estimated that one-fourth of all Scottish financial assets were invested in the company. The colony was to be named New Edinburgh, and the surrounding territory was to be known as New Caledonia.

The slogan of the company was, "Become the door of the two seas and the key to the universe which will enable its proprietors to rule both oceans." It was an incredible and ultimately unworkable goal.

The first expedition left Leith Harbor on July 17, 1698. The fleet included five ships: the *St. Andrew, Unicorn,* and *Caledonia,* each carrying forty-six to seventy guns, and the *Endeavor* and *Dolphin,* which were tenders or yachts laden with provisions, military stores, and merchandise. Toward the end of August, the entire fleet reached the island of Madeira, where their first orders were opened, directing them to call at Crab Island in the vicinity of Puerto Rico. They finally cast anchor on November 2 near a fine natural island four miles east of

Golden Island, off the coast of Darien. The following day, they landed, and "after their hearty thanks to Almighty God for their safe arrival took possession."[1]

A second expedition departed on September 24, 1699, and was sent to reinforce the colony in New Caledonia. That expedition arrived on November 30. The passage had been favorable for wind and weather, but there had been a great deal of sickness. Some 160 persons died on the voyage, including the Rev. Alexander Dalgleish, leaving a sorrowing widow with child. He died between Montserat and Darien.[2]

One can imagine the cries of joy, though, as the colonists from both expeditions saw before them the Golden Island and beyond forests and mountains. It was not gold that occupied their minds but the connection of the two great oceans, the abolition of distance and danger, and the saving of time. This door between seas, the key to the universe, would enable them to be the arbitrators of the commercial world. On that lonely and neglected shore, they imagined a great colony, founded on principles of perfect freedom and trade.[3]

The colonists erected a fort, built huts, and cleared land for planting yams and maize. Agriculture proved difficult, however, and the local Indians were unwilling to barter their combs and other items for food. The torrid, sweltering climate (at 8.30 degrees north of the equator) and inadequate provisions soon caused fever to spread, as well, and many colonists died. The King of England was angry with the Scots' trade initiative and sent instructions to his colony in Jamaica not to resupply the Scottish settlement. The anticipated fleet of merchant ships from the west did not appear laden with cargo from the East

Indies. To make matters worse, the Spaniards claimed Darien to be within their sphere of influence.

In February 1700, a Spanish fleet anchored off Golden Island but withdrew after a meeting of the Spanish commanders with the Scots, who promised that the Indians would remain the subjects of the Spanish king and that the colonists would recognize Spanish sovereignty in the region. The colonists agreed to give the Spanish fourteen days to gather wood and water before they were ready to sail. As soon as the wind was fair, all their ships sailed away. It was clear that the Spanish would prevail.

In April 1700, after just seven months in the harsh tropical climate, the colonists left Darien in seven ships. Five ships arrived safely in Scotland after a three-month layover in Jamaica; one was wrecked near Cartagena, and the *Rising Sun* was sunk in a hurricane off the coast of the British colony of Charles Town, though fifteen colonists survived the shipwreck, including the members of the Stobo family.

### Archibald Stobo and Elizabeth Park

Archibald Stobo was twenty-three years of age and a recently ordained minister of the Church of Scotland when he took the hand of Elizabeth "Betsy" Park, age nineteen, in the tiny St. Margaret's chapel on the grounds of Castle Rock in Edinburgh. The chapel seated barely thirty worshippers. This was a fashionable wedding of two Scots from venerable Scottish families of writers or lawyers.[4] Their wedding was an important event in that small capital city.

The Stobo family's name was not common in Scotland in

those days. The Park's name was connected, however, with Haddington, a village seven miles east of Edinburgh. The Park family prided itself in being distant relatives of the famous Protestant reformer John Knox and his wife, Mary, of that same village. Mary was from the Sinclair family, whose fame is connected with the lovely Roslin Chapel built nearby in 1446 by Sir William Sinclair. During the tense days of the Scottish Reformation in the 1560s, John Knox used the surname "Sinclair" in some of his correspondence when he was being hunted by the ecclesiastical authories.[5] As is still the custom in Scotland, the middle name of a baby girl is often chosen to honor a famous forebear, and Elizabeth Park received the middle name "Sinclair" at her baptism.

Scarcely two months after their wedding, the young couple bade farewell to their families and boarded a ship of the second expedition of Darien adventurers, which sailed on September 24, 1699. Their baby, Jean, was evidently born in Darien just before the colonists abandoned the settlement in April 1700.

Rev. Stobo, Elizabeth, and Jean were among the survivors of the *Rising Sun*. The ship was caught on a reef just off the shore of Charles Town. A small party of fifteen colonists rowed to the shore to get help. They were not able to return, though, since on the night of September 3, 1700, the storm raged so savagely that the remaining 112 persons perished in the sea as the ship fell apart.[6]

Rev. Stobo became the pastor of a small Presbyterian congregation in Charles Town and later founded several churches along the Atlantic coast in the present-day states of South Carolina and Georgia.

Two centuries later, President Theodore Roosevelt claimed to be a descendent through his mother, Martha Bulloch, of the Stobos' daughter, Jean. This claim is recorded in a letter President Roosevelt wrote to the Presbyterian Historical Society. He wrote: "As a matter of fact, I have more Scotch-Irish blood in me even than Dutch."[7]

# 3 | James Collie Sinclair

"Grandpa, I've written up the story you told me last month about William and Barbara. I have done more research about where some of the families of the Calder neighborhood went after the clearances," said Martha. "But I really want you to tell me what happened to the children of William and Barbara after they left Achavarigil and moved to Wick."

"Oh, there are many stories," replied Grandpa. "But the one that you will want to know is the story of Jamie Sinclair. His real name was James Collie Sinclair. He was their eldest son, born in 1798. He signed up as a mercenary soldier and went off to fight against the Spaniards in a far-off country in South America."

"Could that country have been Chile?" asked Martha. "I have a classmate at the University of Edinburgh who told me about the Scots who migrated to South America as merchants, missionaries, soldiers of fortune, and teachers. I especially remember her telling me about a Quaker teacher, Joseph Lancaster, who introduced a new method of teaching down there."

"Yes, it was Chile," Grandpa confirmed. "So you may already know the historical setting for this story. I picked up a few facts in the history books about how things were down there in the early 1800s. Chile was a rebellious Spanish colony and threw off the yoke of Spanish tyranny about that time. A military officer known as the 'Liberator' was driven out of Spain and sailed to Buenos Aires in 1811 to help the rebels in

Argentina. The new independent government there accepted his rank of lieutenant colonel and asked him to recruit and train a cavalry corps known as the Mounted Grenadiers."

"But how is the story related to Chile?" Martha inquired. "There is a huge mountain range between the two countries."

"It was an amazing story of how he took a small army across those mountains to Peru and then down to Chile in 1817," Grandpa responded. "The Chilean rebels had put together a small navy with ships captured from the enemy and bought other boats from England and the United States. It was a risky enterprise, but under the command of an English admiral, Lord Cochrane, and a Chilean officer, Blanco Encalada, they first routed the Spanish army in the north of Chile."

"But how did people like Lord Cochrane show up in Chile?" asked Martha.

"You must remember that the British had maintained a base for their fleet in the Pacific in the port of Valparaíso, so there was a colony of English people there since the early part of that century," Grandpa answered. "However, the Spanish hung desperately to that port. Only an infusion of mercenary soldiers could make the Chilean patriots strong enough to hold the port. It was also a vital link for the patriots to receive arms and munitions to continue their struggle for independence in 1817 and 1818."

"Now I see that it was arrival of the contingent of British mercenaries that tipped the balance from defeat to victory," Martha concluded.

"Let me go back to the reason Jamie joined the Sinclair-Gunn Regiment in 1817. He was only nineteen, and there were not many jobs open to his generation in that small fishing port of Wick, Scotland," explained Grandpa. "He could have worked as an apprentice to his uncle as a stonemason or possibly got a position as a junior clerk in the Mackay General Store. But he had the wanderlust, which was whetted by the stories he heard down at the Seamen's Rest—the gathering place at the harbor for the retired soldiers and sailors who had served in places like Poland, South Africa, and India. He heard the names 'Warsaw,' 'Durban,' and 'Lucknow,' places he had trouble finding on the map. But any place would be more interesting than this boring port with nothing to do but stand around and feel miserable."

### A Notice on the Post Office Door

> WANTED: Volunteers for the Chile detachment of the British Legion. Serve the cause to free a young nation from the Spanish tyrants! The Sinclair-Gunn Regiment will ship out on August llst. Enlistment bonus 20 pounds. Enquire at the desk.

Jamie talked over the decision to join up with his parents and especially with his grandfather, Captain Harrow of Skarferry, who had actually sailed down the east coast of South America as far as Buenos Aires in 1809. According to the old captain, the Spanish were a mean crowd, and their continued control of that part of the world was a menace that also threatened the commerce which Great Britain was developing in that part of the world. In addition, those Spaniards were papists who forbade people from reading the Holy Book. In fact, just that month the pastor of the parish church had read a report to the congregation about a seller of the scriptures who was stoned in Peru.

Further moving Jamie were the romantic tales of the lovely tropical cities that enjoyed an eternal spring. The old sailors at the Seamen's Rest spoke of flowers in the parks year-round and vegetables in abundance. The meat supply for the cities was provided by cattle driven in from the plains every few weeks. Oh, for a chaw of good beef rather than this awful cod Jamie had to eat every day!

By mid-May, he had signed up, been fitted out in his uniform, and finished the basic training at the local armory. He was now Private James C. Sinclair, a fully vetted member of the Sixth Platoon of the Sinclair-Gunn Regiment of the British Legion. There were teary farewells and an earful of counsel from his elders. Captain Harrow pressed into Jamie's hand a small envelope labeled "heather seeds."

"Son, take along some heather seeds," said the captain. "They will probably grow well at that latitude south of the equator. I reckon that you'll be about the same distance from the South Pole as Scotland is from the North Pole."

The French schooner *Liberté* was ready to sail down the Clyde River from the port of Glasgow by late September, and Jamie, in his colorful regimental uniform, was on board. It would be a long and hazardous journey across the Atlantic and down the coast of Brazil to their first port, Recife, Brazil, with its scorching heat. There they took on barrels of fresh water, meat, vegetables, and fruit. The crew seemed renewed for the second leg of their journey. The ship had to chart a course far out at sea since the Spanish fleet was keeping Buenos Aires under siege.

When they reached the tip of South America, the captain chose the shorter and less dangerous route to the Pacific Ocean through the Straits of Magellan, rather than around the Horn. Fortunately, the waters in the straits were relatively calm. Jamie reveled in his first sight of the Chilean mainland, feeling as if he could almost touch the shore as they passed through the narrow channel.

After the schooner *Liberté* emerged from the straits, it faced the vast but calm Pacific Ocean. It was the beginning of summer in that far-off corner of the globe. Soon the ship was joined by a Chilean frigate that guided it into the Port of Valparaíso.

What a sight to see the port city spread out along the shoreline!

It seemed like the buildings flowed up the hills behind the harbor just like a garment covering the lap of a caring mother. Jamie felt a tug at his heartstrings as he remembered his mother, Barbara, whom he left weeping on the wharf back in his homeland.

What lay ahead of him in this new and strange land? Would he survive in battle? Would he find honor and be decorated for his bravery? And would he ever see the heather-covered hills of Caithness again?

No sooner had the Sinclair-Gunn Regiment landed and been quartered—in an old Spanish barracks that the enemy had recently abandoned—when an alarm sounded. The recently departed Spanish fleet was making a last attempt to reoccupy the battery at the far end of the bay.

Quickly, the troops marched along the western arm of

the bay to meet the anticipated landing of the enemy. The initial skirmish was short but bloody, leaving a dozen of his comrades dead and another twenty wounded, and they could not repulse a second attempt by the enemy. But suddenly, a storm swept in from the south that forced the Spaniards to return to their mother ships for the night.

During a tense night watch, a miracle happened that saved the port. A French man-of-war, previously undetected by either friend or foe, suddenly appeared in the early morning light on the far horizon. The Spanish captain immediately saw that he was outgunned and had to withdraw. What could a twenty-cannon ship do against the swifter thirty-cannon master frigate? The city was saved.

The Chilean volunteer army was quite a sight—three hundred mostly barefoot recruits with only light arms. Yet they had a tremendous spirit that made them seem much stronger. The language barrier between the Scots and the Chileans did not make much of a difference, since the Scots believed strongly in the Chileans' right to obtain their freedom, just as they had driven out their English overlords less than a century before.

The mercenary troops were hard pressed because of the initial casualties that their contingent of less than three hundred had suffered in the first encounter with the enemy at the battle of Puente Negro. They had suffered 53 killed, and another 103 lay in a temporary hospital in the old Spanish convent.

Lt. James C. Sinclair wrote his parents:

Dear Ones,

On my first day off guard duty, a group of us climbed

a hill overlooking the bay to pay our respects to our fallen comrades. A plot of ground had been given to the British Legion as a military cemetery. Chaplain John Nicolson led us in prayer as we knelt to pay tribute to the four men who had been my school pals: George Morrison, Alex McKay, William McIver, and Peter McCrae.

God has protected me thus far, and I am well in body. Our Chilean comrades have received us with deep gratitude and warmth. That does not mean that I don't miss terribly my loved ones and friends in Old Wick.

With affection,

Jamie

A group of junior officers were invited by the Williamson family for high tea or *onces* ("elevens"), named after their drink of choice, *aguardiente* (spelled with eleven letters). The Williamson family had come to Chile in 1799 as agents for their trading company based in Glasgow. They invited the Aguilars, their neighbors, to meet their military guests. María Aguilar was seventeen, and she caught the young soldier's eye.

Onces were served on the balcony, from which the guests looked out on the bay and the ocean that stretched out beyond the horizon to New Zealand and Australia. But Jamie was not as interested in the view as he was in the lovely young María, especially in her striking dark eyes and flowing auburn hair. He enjoyed speaking to her in English, even though she interjected a few Spanish words.

"Your parents were kind to invite us into their home and give us such a warm welcome," said Jamie. "I feel like I am back in Wick visiting neighbors down the street. Before I left for Chile, I was told that one can learn any language by just asking two questions."

"And may I ask what those two questions are?" María inquired.

"The first question is, How do you say it? and the second, Will you please repeat it?" he answered.

"You can practice your Spanish on me anytime, soldier," she said as she planted a kiss on his sunburned cheek.

"Como se dice?" he asked.

"Un beso," she replied.

"Hagalo otra vez," he returned.

And with that encouragement she planted a second kiss on his cheek.

"Well didn't you ask for a second kiss!" María laughed. "Now you have learned a third phrase: 'Do it again, Lieutenant Sinclair.'"

And with that she took his hand and led him to a sofa on the balcony to continue their conversation—half in English, half in Spanish.

"María, I really like it here in Chile. It is so much like my native land—sea breezes and sun during the day and cool nights. I know, though, that it gets cold in the winter and plenty hot in the summer. But I really don't look forward to returning to Scotland when this terrible conflict is ended."

"You really don't have to return," offered María. "Perhaps my uncle would have work for you at the trading company.

He is always in need of someone who can handle the English correspondence."

"That's a possibility," he replied. "You have a great family, and of course, I'd enjoy being your friend."

"I hope I can be more than just a new friend," said María. "Perhaps, I could be your special friend. You could teach me more English and tell me more about the independence movement in your homeland."

Months later, Jamie proposed marriage to María in the presence of her adoring parents. An Anglican chaplain married the couple in a simple ceremony in the army's rustic chapel. The spacious Aguilar home became the home of the young couple in the long-established extended family tradition of Latin culture.

Their happiness was ended abruptly by a sharp change in the fortunes of the revolutionary army. Another Spanish invasion on the coast south of Valparaíso called for a quick military response. Jamie was mortally wounded in an ambush that caught the poorly armed troops unaware. He was carried to a field hospital, but survived only a few days. They buried him beside his Scottish comrades. The sorrowing young widow, María Aguilar de Sinclair, had just turned eighteen and was six months pregnant. Their child, born in December 1819, was christened James Sinclair Aguilar.

A letter, translated by a secretary in the Williamson Trading Company office, was sent by María's parents to Jamie's parents in Wick:

Dear parents of your beloved son Jamie:
    It is with heavy hearts that we write to express our

deepest sympathy for the loss of your dear son. He died for the cause of freedom for our beloved country—so weak and vulnerable against the Spanish tyrants. We planted some heather seeds he had brought from Scotland around his gravestone.

We offer on behalf of all Chilean people our deepest gratitude for his sacrifice. We will always remember his gentle manners, sweet smile, and soft speech—even though our mastery of the English language is still limited. Our dear María speaks English much better!

Our darling grandson James is already a cherished member of our family, as he will be of yours. For the present, it seems wise that both María and Jamie, Jr., remain with us since we do not see any way that they can risk at this time the hazardous journey to your country.

Respectfully,

The Aguilar family

A response to this letter came some six months later through the military post:

Dear members of our Chilean family:

Thank you for your dear letter telling us of the death of Jamie and the birth of our new grandson who bears his father's name. You are generous to enfold him into your extended family for the foreseeable future. It is painful for us not to see him. However, it seems wise and prudent for María and our grandson to remain with you in Chile. God may open a way later for them to be united with their Scottish relatives. We will leave that matter in God's Providential Plan.

With affection,

William and Barbara Sinclair

## Afterword

Martha followed up on this story with her friends from Chile. She also spoke with a history professor at the University of Edinburgh who was a specialist in Anglo-Chilean relations to see if he knew of any archival material that might document her descendents now living in Chile. She soon discovered that there were some Sinclair families living in Chile. The contributions of the descendents of Scottish people who settled there is a part of Chile's past and even its present political history. The infamous General Santiago Sinclair, the "hatchet man" of General Pinochet, descended from the early Sinclairs.[1]

In a lighter note, however, lest we take ourselves too seriously as Scots, hear the words of Robert Burns on seeing a louse on a lady's bonnet in church: "O wad some Power the giftie gie us / To see oursels as ithers see us! / It wad frae monie a blunder free us, / An' foolish notion . . . " (from "To a Louse").

## 4 | The Presbyterian and the Buddhist

### Deployment to St. Helena

Kennett Sinclair, as have many young Scots, chose to go to sea. His intention was to serve as an able-bodied seaman aboard one of the coastal commercial vessels that formed the lifeline for the villages and islands of Northern Scotland. Growing up, Kennett had listened to many stories of life at sea from a relative, Captian James Harrow of Skarsferry, Caithness. Though likely born in Caithness, Kennett was reared and educated by his aunt in Inverness, not a port city but still close to the North Sea. No records confirm the relationship of Kennett Sinclair—through his mother, Margaret Harrow—to Captain Harrow, though they have been related through my great-great-grandmother Barbara Harrow.

Thanks to a recommendation that may have come through Sir John Sinclair, secretary of agriculture for Scotland and a friend of Captain Harrow's, Kennett received an appointment to the Royal Naval Academy. Upon his graduation at the age of nineteen, he was ready for an overseas posting. He dreamed of being stationed at some exotic tropical post of the vast British Empire and hoped that he would really see the world.

Little by little, news began to filter through the barracks that Napoleon Bonaparte, the world's most hunted criminal, had

---

The author is indebted to David Mitchell of South Africa for much of the information about Kennett Sinclair and Susana Dell through correspondence found in the author's possession.

been captured by the British naval forces and would be held prisoner on the tiny island of St. Helena in the south Atlantic Ocean, about six thousand miles south of Great Britain and nearly one thousand miles west of the African continent. He was to be held under house arrest in the palatial mansion Longwood House in the custody of His Majesty's Royal Navy.

So it was not to an exotic tropical island in the South Pacific, like Tonga or Pitcairn, that his detachment was to be sent but to the isolated St. Helena (also known as the "Rock") to guard this illustrious criminal. The naval schooner *Ensign Royal* carried a crew of fifteen and the naval detachment of twenty men and two officers on the long voyage south. They stopped in port only once, in the Azores, for two days to resupply the ship. The voyage seemed endless as the ship followed the Southern Cross at night and the compass was set on due south during the day. At last, St. Helena loomed high and clear on the far horizon.

St. Helena Island was discovered by the Portuguese in 1502. The island was named after St. Helena, the mother of Constantine the Great. She held a special place of honor as the protector of the Church of the Holy Sepulcher in Jerusalem. The Portuguese built a chapel and some dwellings, but essentially the island was held only as a supply station for the merchant fleet. The early settlers introduced goats as a source of meat, planted fruit trees, and cultivated gardens to supply the ships.

Never truly settled by the Portuguese, the island was eventually used as a base for the trading operations of the East India Company for their ships en route to the East Indies. This lonely place, an island of volcanic origin, became the home to people of many races.

## Kennett and Susanna Meet and Marry

Despite the presence of the infamous prisoner, life was very dull on that lonely outpost of the Empire. The inhabitants were farmers and herdsmen, a few shopkeepers, servants, the naval detachment, and the crew of the *Ensign Royal*. One family seemed, however, to take interest in the British military group. The following story may have taken place in Kennett's life, as East met West on that far-off island.

The Dell family was descended from Malaysians brought to South Africa in the 1680s as indentured servants. After they had completed their labor contracts, they were free to settle wherever they chose. A position was advertised for an English-speaking agent to manage a store that sold staple goods and cloth to a small clientele on this military outpost. The agent could take his family with him. The family applied for the position: father, mother, niece, and nephew. They became the unofficial hosts to the British garrison. Their distinctive speech, customs, dress, and demeanor set them apart from the rest of the population. But this lonely island soon became their home, and they never thought of returning to South Africa, much less to Malaysia. Nearly everyone on the island knew them since their general store was the place where most of the commerce was transacted.

It was Kennett's day off guard duty. He needed to buy some casual garb since the military men were exempt from wearing their uniforms when off duty. The cook of the detachment was an East Indian who suggested that there were some good prices at the store operated by his uncle Rakim.

A lovely twenty-eight-year-old woman (described in the

records as "a white lady from Cape Town") with a graceful and poised manner, clipped British speech, and an air of confidence waited on him. Her demeanor was different from that of the more submissive native women of the island. He overheard her name, Susanna, spoken by her uncle as he added up the bill for his purchase.

Kennett returned the next week after he had received his pay to make an additional purchase. He greeted the young woman by name. She was surprised.

"How did you know my name, sir?" Susanna asked.

"Pardon my familiarity," Kennett replied, "but I overheard your uncle use your name."

"Oh, that's alright," she returned. "We Malaysians feel more at home with you Scots than with the cold English people. I consider it evidence of your friendship that you used my first name. And, sir, may I inquire as to your Christian name?"

"It is not an ordinary Scottish name . . . Kennett, but I like it nonetheless," he answered.

It was not many weeks until Kennett cautiously approached Uncle Rakim to ask permission to visit his niece in their home. In that clime, there were long evenings, just as in Scotland. Uncle Rakim knew that sooner or later his niece would marry someone. Why not take a chance with a decent, clean-shaven sailor?

Kennett called on Susanna one Saturday evening in the company agent's living quarters. Uncle Rakim ushered him into a sitting room where Susanna was waiting. Then he disappeared behind a curtain in the adjoining drawing room. There would be little that would escape his notice.

The conversation was a bit stilted at first as Kennett referred to an image—a fat figure, both jolly and serious looking—placed in a shrine on the wall with some flowers and a small dish with burning incense.

"Oh, that's a Buddha," Susanna said, "but we don't really pay much attention to him. We've been away from the temple in South Africa where I grew up and don't think much about religion out here. I presume you are a Christian. Aren't there many kinds of Christians? Which kind are you?"

"I am a Presbyterian and a member of the Church of Scotland," Kennett responded. "We don't have any statues in our churches. We read from the Holy Scriptures and sing the Psalms of David in our worship. Our pastors are married and live a lot like the rest of us."

"Oh, yes, I know about the Presbyterians since my school girlfriend in Cape Town is the daughter of a pastor," she explained. "They are nice people. Once I went to her church the day she became a member—you know, when the young people are old enough to drink the wine and eat the bread they serve on special occasions."

"Susanna, I am relieved to hear you say that you know something about Presbyterians. I am relieved since I thought my religion might hurt our friendship," he said.

"Oh, don't give that another thought," reassured Susanna. "You are a good person and I feel comfortable talking with you."

During the rest of the conversation, Kennett was thinking about the words of a poem he once heard. It was about a British soldier who fell in love with a Buddhist girl in Mandalay. It was about "the girl who worshipped an idol made of mud that they called 'the Great God Budd.'" Was that this idol on the shelf—a Buddha?

"I still would like to give her a big hug and 'kiss her where she stands,' as the poem says," he thought. Then his thoughts turned back to the conversation, even though Susanna probably wondered why he was silent for a few moments.

Susanna and Kennett were about the same age. Immediately, they found much to talk about—culture, language, and life experiences. Of course, later in their courtship there were those intimate conversations that are common to every clime where there is twilight and moonlight.

Kennett was madly in love with Susanna. But how could he break away from the racial prejudices of his Scottish heritage? He remembered vividly the Gordon family that lived down the street in Inverness. Their soldier son married a servant girl from a household where he was billeted in Egypt. His parents were so upset that they wrote to their son and told him that he should not return with his bride to Scotland, because of the racial discrimination she would have to endure.

This matter worried Kennett, as he wrote to his mother, asking for her counsel:

Dear Mother,

I have fallen in love with a woman of Malaysian descent—a Buddhist by birth but I believe she is a Christian in her heart. I can not hide from my dear mother the thought that this news may distress you. We Scottish people harbor much prejudice toward people of other races. But I am sure that you would certainly

love her as a daughter, yet it would be hurtful for her
to live in a Scottish community. Her parents have given
permission for our marriage, and the Anglican chaplain
will perform the religious service. What is your counsel to me as one whom I love dearly?

My military service obligation will end in another
six months here on St. Helena. Susanna has relatives in
the Cape, where we can live while I seek employment
in South Africa.

My love as always, your devoted son,

Kennett

The following answering letter came in a matter of
months, but by then Kennett and Susanna were married, settled
in South Africa, and awaiting the birth of their first child:

Our dearest son,

This is a difficult letter to write. I wish we were
closer so we could talk over your decision to marry
Susanna. You have rightly assessed the racial prejudice
that still reigns among our neighbors here in Inverness,
even though we do not share their feelings.

My counsel to you is that you wait awhile before
taking this step. Think carefully about the future for
yourself, Susanna, and your children. We trust that you
will accept this thought that is born out of our true
love for you and your future.

With affection,

Mother

The descendents of Kennett and Susanna in South Africa may someday be found in a South African archive. Good starting points for such a genealogical search might include: Thomas Sinclair (1818–1900); David Sinclair, his son (1860–1935); Della, his granddaughter (1895–1960); Andrew Mitchell, her husband (1894–1980); Thomas Sinclair Mitchell, their son (1924–2000); David Sinclair Mitchell, their son (1930–); and Alexander Sinclair Mitchell, his son (1980–).

The heather seed has now been scattered in South Africa for two centuries. Seven generations of Sinclairs and their kin form part of the Celtic and Anglo-Saxon racial strains of modern South Africa. East and West, North and South are blended in that nation: Scot, Malaysian, English, Dutch, Boer, Afrikaner, and African. South Africans truly can be called a global race.

# 5 | A Family Scandal Scatters Sinclairs to Venezuela and Canada

Donald Gillies was born in 1775 into a Highland family that had settled in Aberdeen in the early part of the century. He was a master mechanic in the Paton Woolen Mills, a member of the Scottish Rite Masonic Order, and an office bearer in the Church of Scotland. He served in the army for nine years in the 1790s.

Fiona Sinclair, his spouse, had come to Aberdeen as a domestic servant in the employ of the Paton family. Her ancestral roots were in the Calder neighborhood near Halkirk, Caithness. She had married Donald when she was eighteen. They met when the mill owner used his services in the Paton manor house to repair the mechanical elevator that lifted the food from the kitchen to the dining hall.

Donald and Fiona married and established their first home in a working-class section of Aberdeen in 1806. To this happy union were born five children: John, Donald, Duncan, Margaret, and Angus. The family was blessed with adequate wages, good food, spiritual nourishment in the parish church, and a pleasant life in a peaceful neighborhood.

All seemed to be going well. John, now eighteen, was an apprentice to his uncle at the woolen mill and living the routine life of an urban factory worker. On Sunday afternoon a group of young men, accompanied at times by some young ladies, would picnic down by the Dee River. John was certainly interested in looking for a wife. His sweetheart was Sally, the daughter of the foreman of the factory, Sandy McLeod.

John would linger with Sally on the riverbank in the evening hours as long as they thought they could get away with it, and eventually, Sally became pregnant. A hush-hush story traveled around the neighborhood that the father of the child was a shady lad from the country, but John soon confessed that he was Sally's lover and the father of the child. He was willing to marry Sally, but her family would not hear of it, because she would be marrying below her station.

Sally was quietly shipped off to her grandmother's in Edinburgh. The baby was born there and adopted as a member of her grandmother's extended family. The city was large, and she had many relatives who circled around to dote over her child.

Sally found work in a local bakery. She loved the more exciting life of a big city and soon found a new suitor, the bakery owner's son. Letters were sent back and forth to and from her parents about her future. But she was now eighteen and on her own, and she was determined to marry her new boyfriend. When John saw that Sally no longer cared for him, he reluctantly signed over his paternal rights to Sally and her future husband.

The Gillies family was more than just embarrassed over the incident; they felt shunned by the factory families and even by some of the church families. How could they get away from Aberdeen?

Donald read aloud to Fiona a notice in the morning's paper: "Openings for shepherds, gardeners, blacksmiths, master mechanics, and other artisans. Join the Caledonian Development Company in a promising agricultural and industrial project in Venezuela, South America. Inquiry at 65 Mackay Street, Aberdeen."

"Anywhere far away from Aberdeen will be right for me," replied Fiona. "Go down and see if you would qualify for the mechanic's job. Ask them about the conditions and how long the contract would last. Tell them that two of our sons are sixteen and eighteen and that they're good workers."

Donald returned with a brochure that gave many details about the colonization project. It explained that the Topo Project was not far from the capital city of Caracas and the nearby port of La Guaira in Venezuela. The company had purchased a large tract of land where indigo would be grown, which was used in the dark red dye at the woolen mills. The indigo plants would be milled there and shipped back to Scotland, making up for the dye that could no longer be brought in from the East Indies because of the French and Spanish blockade of the Mediterranean Sea.

"Look here, too. It says that the company will provide our passage, victuals aboard ship, lessons in Spanish, and the opportunity to buy fifty acres of land over the first five years," explained Donald. "The agent I talked with was Mr. John Ross, who, I remember, used to be the parish minister at St. George's church before he became a Parliament reporter down in London."

"Most of it sounds good, but our daughter might fall in love with one of those natives down there," worried Fiona.

"Don't worry about that, because there will be at least forty families of Scots signing up for the project," he reassured. "There should be some eligible young bachelors among the settlers."

They discussed the advantages and disadvantages of the venture with their children, relatives, and neighbors. They were promised an annual wage of two hundred pounds and housing and provisions for the eight months until the first crop was harvested. The first group of colonists would set sail on October 1, 1825, out of the Port of Glasgow on a 600-ton frigate that the company had built in Amsterdam.

The decision was soon made, although the younger children said they would miss their friends at school. They rented their small home to a relative, packed up the old family trunks, gave away their pets, and were given a tearful farewell at the parish church hall.

The voyage to Venezuela lasted nearly three weeks, with only one port stop at Funchal in the Madeira Islands. Among the forty families, 198 people were onboard: 45 men, 57 women, and 96 children. The settlers were instructed to be friendly, respectful, and modest toward the Venezuelans. Most of the colonists were Protestants who would be living in a Catholic land, so they would need to be cautious in their comments about religious matters. They had been assured, however, that the laws of the new nation of Gran Colombia guaranteed full religious freedom to non-Catholics if their services were held indoors.

When they arrived at the Topo Plantation, the colonists were first housed in barracks with some sixty rooms that had been built for the settlers. They had arrived too late to plant their first crops during the rainy season, but the company promised them rations for the first six months.[1]

The land that had been purchased for the indigo plantation

included 724 acres of cultivated land and many more acres of bordering wasteland. These bordering lands were rocky and good only for goat grazing. The plantation was set in an upland valley about six miles long, located between the humid heat of the Caracas valley about eight miles to the southeast and the torrid heat of La Guaira five miles to the northeast. Tuna cactus, cocuy, and thornbushes grew on the arid slopes. A small creek that ran through the valley had been dammed at intervals for irrigation. Coffee trees had been planted in a few fertile areas, but they would not bear fruit for five years. The land was said, however, to be optimal for the cultivation of the indigo plant (*Indigofera tinctoria*).

The land agent had greatly exaggerated the land's fertility for both farming indigo and providing grains and pasture for the forty families. The settlers found that they could not even make a down payment on the land with their meager earnings. The agent in La Guaira threatened to withhold their rations unless they made their payments. He was being hard-pressed by the London office owing to the financial crisis of 1825. The settlers found themselves between a rock and a hard place.

The leader of the Topo colony, John Ross, was not up to the task of leadership. He was as disappointed as the rest of the colonists but chose to drown his frustration in alcohol rather than face the situation. His frequent drinking bouts were made worse by the ready availability of the rum produced by the nearby sugar plantation.

Hunger soon threatened the little colony. Six members of the colony, including Donald Gillies, appealed to Sir Robert Ker Porter, the British consul in Caracas. Thirty-four of the settlers also sent a petition to Parliament asking for help immigrating to the United States or Canada. Only the intervention of Joseph Lancaster—a Quaker educator who worked with General Simón Bolívar in developing the new nation's educational system—saved the colony. He was able to raise money from some wealthy citizens and a five-hundred-pesos donation from General Bolívar to keep the Topo settlers alive.[2]

A glimmer of hope came in early 1826 when the Emigration Committee of the British parliament reported plans for a new settlement in Canada. The consul was relieved when he received this word and contacted his brother who was in public service in Quebec. The consul had more important matters before him and wanted to get these disgruntled Scots off his hands. Soon, arrangements were made to ship the several hundred settlers off to Canada by way of Philadelphia, New York, and Buffalo.

The colonists left in two contingents. The first, known as the Butchart party, arrived in New York City and included Donald and Fiona Gillies and their four children. There they were met by the British consul, but he had received no instructions on how to get them to Canada nor what help would be waiting for them once they arrived. Seventy-four people were in the group, representing eleven families, and he did not want them on his hands. So he shipped them up the Hudson River to Albany and by canal boat to Buffalo. The settlers then traveled by boat across the lake to Burlington Bay, seventy miles from the land offered by the Canada Company at the site of the newly surveyed city of Guelph.

The Gillies family of six spent the first months living in a

tent, and the men found employment building roads and clear-
ing the land for cabins. The administrator of the project, John
Galt, was not a good administrator and was accused of poor
accounting of the funds he had received "to help the Guayr-
ians," as the Topo settlers were called. He was recalled by the
company in 1829.

The new agent of the Canada Company was struck with
compassion at the plight of these families with sickly women
and children. There were thirty-seven children under the age
of fourteen. Most were suffering from ague and malaria and in
need of medical attention. He was able to provide them with
pork, sugar, tea, flour, and tobacco, as well as kettles and baking
pans. A start was made at erecting the frames of cabins that the
settlers would need to finish before winter set in. The children
were sent to school. A community began to form amid the stress
and strain of finding a home in a new land. At last the Topo settlers saw some hope.

Imagine a tract of one million acres with a population of
three hundred souls. Only a seventy-mile bridle path through
the forest connected the settlement with the outside world
beyond Lake Huron. There were no bridges, no mill, and no
industry, only a trackless forest in this vast untamed land. They
gave, however, a royal name to their motley cluster of rustic
dwellings—Guelph—the name of a branch of the Hanoverian
dynasty of the British Empire.[3]

Today the city of Guelph is listed as one of Canada's most
livable cities because of its clean environment, low crime rate,
and generally high standard of living. The University of Guelph,
founded in 1873, is one of the nation's top universities. The city

is the home of Ontario's agricultural college and veterinarian school. Because of its location and accessibility by public transportation, it is often the site of national academic meetings.

Imagine a conversation that two academics, one a native of Guelph and the other a psychology professor from Manitoba, may have had at a national conference at the University of Guelph in 2009.

"Yours is one of the more numerous Scottish clan names in Canada. The Sinclairs seem to show up everywhere!" exclaimed Professor Gillie.

"You can say that again," replied Professor Lisa Sinclair, chair of the Department of Applied Psychology at the University of Manitoba. "My dad told me that my great-uncle Henderson Sinclair came from Caithness in 1910. He was a descendent of a William Sinclair and Barbara Harrow, who were married in Halkirk, Caithness, in 1795."

"That's interesting. I'm descended from one of the Scottish settlers who founded Guelph in 1827," responded Professor Gillie. "They came here by way of Venezuela, where they were part of a failed colonization scheme. Apparently, one of my ancestors was a Sinclair from Halkirk, Caithness."

Later in the conference they picked up their conversation.

"I was home over the weekend and talked with one of my older relatives who knows the family history," said Professor Gillie. "He showed me the marriage certificate of a Fiona Sinclair who married a Gillie from Inverness in 1806. According to that record, she was born in Halkirk, where your great-great-great-grandparents came from. A few generations back, we're both probably related to those Sinclairs!"

# 6 | The Adventures of George Sinclair in the Down Under

### George Sinclair Turns His Life Around

The Protestant Reformation of the 1560s never completely changed the religious scene in Northern Scotland, as it did in Glasgow, Edinburgh, and St. Andrew's. The Church of Rome reacted strongly and continued to flourish in the Highlands. A separate college was established in Rome to prepare priests in the Gaelic language, which was spoken by most people in the north. The Church of Scotland continued to maintain its traditional parishes; the landlords served on the kirk sessions and supported the church with their private contributions. The soul of the Highlands had not been deeply changed by the Protestant Reformation.

The Church of Scotland was further weakened in 1740 when four hundred Gaelic-speaking clergy walked out of the general assembly and formed the Free Church of Scotland. This schism was followed by decades of litigation over the properties of divided congregations, each group claiming to be the legitimate owners of their church buildings and lands.

In light of these religious realities, there was space for new denominations to thrive in Scotland. The Baptists and the Congregationalists launched evangelistic efforts to fill the void. The Baptists were particularly successful in Caithness, where a congregation was founded in 1765. One of the founding members was the Earl of Caithness, Sir William Sinclair. He actually traveled to London to be baptized by immersion and formally admitted to the new denomination. He became a lay preacher and held services all over Caithness with great zeal during many years. He wrote and published hymns that are still sung in Baptist congregations.

George Sinclair, son of William and Barbara Sinclair of Halkirk, was named the town marshal in the nearby village of Keiss. Unfortunately, he had become a drunkard in his early years yet was able to hang on to his job. His parents approached the pious Sir William seeking his help to save their wayward son. They hoped that the noble earl, austere but approachable, would confront George about his drinking problem.

Sir William visited with the young police officer in the city hall and spoke to him sternly: "Young man, if you don't change your ways, you'll not only lose your job, you'll give the Sinclairs a bad name. Didn't you hark to the motto of our clan: 'Commit thy work to God'? You're a disgrace to your family, your clan, and your God. I tell you, straighten out your life now before it's too late."

George was impressed that the highly revered Sir William would take an interest in a humble city employee. The two had more conversations, and George listened to many sermons, sitting in the back pew of the little Baptist chapel. In 1833, the thirty-five-year-old George turned his life over to God and stood up to give his testimony before the congregation.

"Pastor, I want to turn my life over to Jesus and follow him. Please pray for me."

George knew that he would have to get away from his old drinking pals and start a new life in some other place. Sir William told him that there was an opening in the Twentieth Foot Regiment, which was scheduled to sail from Ireland the next month for Australia. This unit had been summoned to duty as the armed guard for a ship loaded with Irish rebels who were being transferred (in reality, deported) for life to that far-off corner of the British Empire. George, a bachelor and in fairly good health, enlisted.

The hiring clerk in Wick, who knew about George's past life, was quite frank with him: "George, around here we all know about you and your past, but now you're a good Protestant, and you'll keep them rebel Irish papists in line!"

George was soon off to the Port of Glasgow and then by boat to the Port of Cobb in Ireland. There, he boarded the convict transport *Pamela,* a 443-ton barque under the command of a Scot, Captain James Anderson. He was no virgin captain, since he had already made several trips Down Under with convicts. On the previous voyage he had taken 153 male convicts, with only 5 dying en route. On this voyage he would have to cram 170 prisoners into the same space, which meant less sleeping space than the usual eighteen inches for each convict.[1]

There was a separate deck for the prisoners with a strong barricade spiked with iron built at the steerage bulkhead, giving the guards a view of all that went on among the prisoners. The only exit was through a door that was always guarded. The only relief from claustrophobia were the scuttles, or portholes, above the benches, which could be opened in mild weather.

The voyage from Cobb to Tasmania (then known as Van Diemen's Land) took six weeks. At the first port stop in Bermuda, three of the convicts stole a boat and started to row away to North America. But they were quickly brought back and flogged on the breakwater as the assembled convicts and crew observed their punishment.

After a nearly two-month voyage, the *Pamela* docked in the Port of Hobart. The prisoners were onboard the fifty-two-ton *Kangaroo,* which took them to probation station on the north side of Maria's Island.

There, the prisoners were lodged in the newly erected penal facility of Darlington, which stood on a spit of land beneath twin mountains named the Bishop and the Clerk. The topography of the strange new land actually reminded George of the Highland coast of Caithness, especially the Giant Causeway near his home town of Keiss.

George's first letter to his parents related the surroundings and prospects of his new life Down Under.

Dear Parents,

It has been a long voyage to this new land, but I must admit that we are now in a beautiful place. It even reminds me of some parts around my homeland. Yet the thought of the bleak future of these convicts saddens my heart. There are 130 convicts in Darlington Detention Center, some wearing grey and others, yellow-chequered black—magpie suits reserved for the second-time offenders. The probation here is for five years. If there are no charges brought against them, they will be free to settle permanently here but are prohibited from ever setting foot on British soil anywhere else in the world.

I must admit that this is a lovely place, and once I
finish my tour of duty with the regiment, I think that
I might find a job and a future here. I am well and
keep busy with my duties.

I miss you and love you dearly.

Your son,

George

After George completed his military contract, he teamed
up with another soldier who was also mustered out and settled in Port Arthur. They bought a tract of pastureland to raise
merino sheep, which had just been introduced into Australia.
The climate and pasture were suitable for the wool industry.
A Scot, John Macarthur, had made connections for exporting
the wool to the fourteen Glasgow-based importers. The future
looked sure, but within a couple seasons the transportation
system became too costly. The ocean voyage was long, and the
wool produced nearer to Britain slowly got the corner on the
world wool market. George and his partner had to cash in their
chips and get out of the wool business.

George now needed not only another job but a life partner—a wife—and far too many men were looking for marriageable ladies. According to 1835 colonial government statistics, the
population of 12,836 in Western Australia included only 4,300
women. This situation existed despite the recruitment of a large
group of unattached young Scottish women and the offer of a
twelve-pound bounty payable to them upon arrival. Many of
these women were between the ages of fifteen and thirty-five
and were recommended by the minister of their parish.

## George Sinclair Finds a Wife

The year was 1890 when Grandmother Patty Sinclair told her granddaughter Martha MacClintock the story of her arrival in Australia, the sad events in the life of her birth family, and how she met George Sinclair at Saint Anne's Home, an orphanage for girls and young women known locally as the "Female Factory." Patty was seventy, and Grandpa George had died more than twelve years before when he was seventy-nine. He died in his home county of Caithness in Scotland when he was visiting his relatives. Martha had been very close to her Grammy but only knew her Grandpa George from the photo of the handsome young soldier in his military garb that hung over the fireplace. She knew that he had come to Australia as a British soldier and settled in the sheep business near Dunedin, New Zealand, in the 1840s.

"Grammy, how did you meet Grandpa George?" Martha asked.

"My dear one, that was a long, long time ago," Patty replied. "I was only twenty-three years of age when he came one Sunday afternoon to the orphanage where I lived."

"But why weren't you living with your family?" Martha wanted to know.

Patty explained: "That is a very, very sad story. You are old enough now, however, that you can understand how bad things happen in families when they are new to a country. Our parents were trying to make a home for themselves and a future for their children.

"It was in the year 1833 that our family came to Australia aboard the ship *Pamela*. My father, James Anderson, was the captain of the ship, which was loaded with hundreds of Irish prisoners being transported to Australia because they had gotten into trouble with the British king. They were really not bad people but were Irish and hated being governed by the English.

"Our family had a special cabin on the ship. There were six of us: father, mother, my three sisters, and myself. I was the eldest child and was twelve years of age. The voyage was a long trip that took over three months.

"Everything was going well, and we were just getting settled in our new home in Australia near the army barracks. We were starting school, happy to discover interesting places, and making new friends. But then something happened that changed everything. My father was taken off to jail one day because they said that he had not reported correctly on the money he had received from the government to feed and clothe the Irish prisoners on the voyage from Ireland to Australia. Of course, we all knew that he was being wrongly accused. Our father would never have cheated anyone!

"But we never saw our father again after that day when they took him away in chains. Our mother was grief stricken. We had no relatives or friends in this strange land. What was to happen to us? The local priest helped us for a few weeks, but finally he told our mother that the girls would have to be placed into an orphanage for girls called St. Anne's Home. Our mother would have to return to her parents in Ireland or to her in-laws in Scotland."

"But, Grammy, the government couldn't do that to your father without a trial to prove that he was either guilty or innocent. Why didn't your family get a lawyer?" Martha asked.

"My dear, the country was so young that there were few laws written and courts organized to defend the innocent when they were accused," Patty responded. "We had no place to turn to get justice. The priest told us that all he could do was make sure the children would be protected in the orphanage."

"So your mother tried to find a way to get back to Ireland, and you girls were put in the orphanage," said Martha. "Tell me what that place was like. I think you told us once that it was also called the 'Female Factory.' That doesn't sound like a very nice place."

"It wasn't very nice," Patty replied, "but it was all that there was for us. We were treated just like homeless children. They gave us rations of food, soap, and clothing. It was very simple living. We lived four girls to a room with just a straw mattress on a cot and one blanket each."

"Did your Mother and friends every come to see you?" asked Martha.

"Yes, we could have visitors on Sunday afternoon for two hours," said Patty. "Mother could only come when she could get off work as a nanny. Then there were some young men who came to visit, mostly looking for a young lady they might want to marry."

"And that was how you met Grandpa George?" Martha inquired.

"There was no question that most of the girls wanted to get away from that awful place," Patty answered. "You are right to think that we were all carefully looking over the young men who came to visit. Each of us thought that they might want to marry and take us away to a more pleasant life—anywhere but there."

"Please tell me more. Had you known any of the young bachelors who came to visit?" Martha asked.

"Now that's the most important part of the story. Your Grandpa George had been one of the soldiers on the ship *Pamela,* and he remembered me as one of the daughters of Captain Anderson," Patty replied. "He was much, much older than me. In fact he was nearly forty-five years old, and I was only twenty-two. He was so handsome and seemed in some ways like a father. He seemed interested in me, and we talked a lot about that long voyage from Ireland to Australia when I was only twelve."

"Did he propose to you when he came to visit on Sunday afternoon?" Martha asked.

"Well, not exactly then, but on another occasion when we were able to get together by ourselves, he did. Then we had to wait awhile to get permission to marry, but it all worked out. After we were married and had our first child, your uncle Patrick, we moved to New Zealand. George was a good man, and we had a very happy life together. I still miss him very much."

### The Real Story, Which Was Not Generally Known

St. Anne's Home was formed to care for the many unattached young women who might fall into prostitution unless a refuge was provided for their protection and care. The bishop assigned an order of sisters to establish this home. The women who found refuge there were put into three categories: the first were women who were marriageable; the second were those who had a past relationship that might hinder a second marriage; and the third were women with a criminal record. They lived in cells, five by six feet. Each category of women had a different ration: the more fortunate ones received beef and vegetables with salt, brown sugar, a quarter ounce of tea, and a quarter ounce of yellow soap. Those in category two received one-half that ration, and those in category three received even less.

One can only imagine the tensions among the women in the Factory. They divided into the deserving, the less deserving, and the undeserving, which created a class system that bred infighting and jealousy. It was not a happy situation. Above all, Patty Anderson had been placed their at age twenty against her will. She was desperate to find a way out.

There were occasional garden parties to which certain selected young bachelors were invited. It was only by invitation and with the proper recommendations that young men could attend. George had a friend, however, who knew someone at the Factory who was able to get him an invitation. George met Patty at this garden party, and amid the bustle, they sat in one of the few spaces reserved for quiet conversation.

"Why, I think we have met before," said George. "Aren't you the eldest daughter of Captain Anderson of the ship *Pamela?* I was a member of the armed guard for the Irish prisoners. Why, that was nearly ten years ago."

"Sir, my name is Patty Anderson, at your service," she replied and primly curtsied.

"I am George Sinclair of Keiss, Caithness, also at your

service," George replied. "And may I ask about how things have gone with you since last we traveled together?"

"Sir, please don't ask me that since you know that I wouldn't be in this awful place unless something terrible had happened to my family," she firmly declared.

"Oh, pardon my question. I should have been more prudent in my speech," he apologized.

"Don't give it a thought, soldier," she smiled. "Let's sit down, and you can tell me about yourself and how have things gone with you."

"Well, I've had my ups and downs, like most soldiers who have mustered out after they have served out their contract. I tried sheep ranching for a while, but that didn't work out. Now I'm a watchman at a local factory and just trying to make ends meet," George explained.

The conversation ended rather abruptly when a bell indicated that the party was over and the guests should prepare to leave.

"Mister George, please come back again and let's talk some more about that horrible voyage on the *Pamela*. I'll tell you how I ended up in this place."

Patty felt good about this chance encounter with someone who had known her and her family. She was also pleased that a gallant older man had showed an interest in her. Perhaps he might come back.

George came back as often as he could get an invitation. He and Patty found much to talk about. But how could they get the privacy to do more than just hold hands and sneak in a casual embrace? Their conversation turned also to religion since she was a Roman Catholic and he professed a different faith—he was a Protestant. The sisters had warned the girls to "beware of those heretics."

"George, they say that you Protestants don't believe in God and will all go to hell. Is that true?" Patty asked. "If you're going to hell, I'd like to go there with you!"

"Now, Patty, don't believe that nonsense. We are Christians just like you. We have the same Bible and love the same Jesus," George assured her. "The Holy Bible tells us that God loves everyone. There's a verse in the Gospel of John that goes like this: 'For God so loved the world that He gave His only begotten son, so that whoever believes in Him will have everlasting life.' That means that God loves everybody, just as much as God loves you and me—Baptists, Catholics, and even Sergeant Morrison, who said he was an atheist!"

"George, I like that verse. Is that really in the Holy Book? You say that you have a Bible and read it every night. I have never had the Holy Book even in my hand. Could you bring yours next time so I can actually see it and hold it?"

"Patty, my love, sure, I'd be glad to bring it. But it's not just what the Bible says but the love that God wants everyone to know that is really important. Don't you think that is what religion is all about?"

The months went by, and Patty and George were falling deeper and deeper in love. They wanted to have time just to themselves, but under the watchful eyes of the chaperons, there were only moments for a short embrace and a stolen kiss. How could they arrange a secret meeting?

Nelly, the matron's assistant, was an acquaintance of

George's soldier buddy Peter. She seemed to be the right person to make possible such a meeting. Peter approached her with an offer of twenty pounds if she could arrange a secret midnight tryst in the garden of the Factory. The plan was simply that she would leave the back garden gate unlocked on a certain day and hour. The only condition was that Patty would lock the gate upon her return.

And so the date and hour was arranged and the twenty-pound note paid in advance. Patty and George met that night under a tropical moon and enjoyed the elixir of love to the full.

It seemed these secret meetings happened more than once, and the inevitable happened. Patty began to miss her period and knew she was surely pregnant.

The priest who heard her confession simply asked, "And who might be the father of your anticipated child?"

She trembled as she blurted out, "Why his name is George Sinclair, and he wants to marry me. But he's a Protestant!"

The priest replied without hesitation, "My child, you are a good Catholic woman, and a marriage to a Protestant would not be recognized by the church. Your child would be a bastard. Don't you know that in this place it is forbidden for a Catholic to marry a Protestant?"

Patty had prepared her answer before the confession. She replied in a flash, "But George knows someone who will marry us."

Father Joe replied with controlled anger, "My child, you're a good Catholic woman, and that marriage will not be valid. Your child will be a bastard."

Several weeks went by, and it was George's turn to confess. He approached the matron of the orphanage and handed her a written note:

Dear Madam,

I am the father of the child that is being carried by Patty Anderson. I will take full responsibility for her and the protection of our child. Please trust me and release her to my care.

Respectfully,

George Sinclair

Soon, the marriage was arranged through a payment by a friend to a newly arrived priest who was not related yet to any particular parish but had registered with the diocesan office. The priest tried to extract from George a promise that any children born from this union would be raised in the Roman Church. George said that he would never sign any such agreement. The marriage took place, however, and was duly registered with the county records clerk. George found work in a nearby town, and they rented a small cottage.

In the fall of 1842, a baby boy was born and given the name John Patrick. They had decided that they would not have the baby baptized but would just raise him to be a Christian and forgo the formality. George recalled an understanding that was current in Scotland in those days: a male heir would be raised in the religion of his father; a female child, in the religion of her mother. They had not heard of the *no temere* decrees of the Holy Father in Rome, which stated that

Protestants and Catholics could only be validly married with a special authorization from the Vatican.

Word came to the bishop's office that a child had been born to a mixed marriage and that the couple had decided not to baptize the child. True to his Irish resentment against the Protestant heretics, the bishop filed a court case to order the baby taken from the couple and placed in a Catholic orphanage. The legal code in this new nation had not been defined on this issue. A friendly Protestant lawyer advised them that they would lose the case even if they had the money to fight the legal battle. There was only one way out—leave Australia. But where would they go?

George had a relative, a member of the Free Church of Scotland, who had emigrated from Wick to Dunedin, New Zealand, in one of the first boat loads of Free Church settlers who had gone there in 1841. Perhaps he could advise them if they had a chance of keeping their baby if they moved to another British colony. It was a far-out chance but worth a try.

An army buddy who was to be transferred to the garrison in Dunedin offered to contact the relative, Drew McKenzie, to find out if George Sinclair could move to New Zealand, find a job, and be free from the stigma of being in a mixed marriage that afflicted his family in Australia.

Within a few months, word came back through the military post that there was a sheep herder's opening in the Dunedin area, with a humble dwelling provided for the family.

"Come along," wrote Drew. "We New Zealanders are more liberal when it comes to religion. You will not be harassed here since we Protestants are in the clear majority."

The move was just right in many ways. Patty found a
spiritual home in the local Roman Catholic parish. The Scottish priest only inquired if their child had been baptized but
said nothing more when they replied: "We have agreed just to
raise him as a Christian and let him decide when he grows up
if he wants to go to church with me or with his father to the
Free Church."

Life went well for the Sinclairs in the sheep herder's
job. Soon, they had saved enough to buy a small ranch and
begin their own business. By the early 1860s, when John was
about sixteen, he was drawn to the youth group in his father's
church and became a member of the Free Church. Mother
Patty, though inwardly disappointed, did not object but rather
was pleased that they had reared a fine, upstanding young man
of whom his parents could be proud.

The years of the 1860s and 1870s rolled by quickly. John
Patrick Sinclair purchased his own ranch and married a Presbyterian lass, Sara MacClintock. It was their daughter, Margaret,
who married Ross MacDonald in 1910. Their son, Paul, graduated from the University of Dunedin in 1934 and was chosen to
prepare to become a faculty member with a scholarship at the
University of California in Berkeley. The Sinclair-MacDonald
saga continued through the friendship of Paul MacDonald and
Dr. Eileen Marie Sinclair, a professor at the University of Manitoba, who met when they were in graduate school in San Francisco in 1938.

# 7 | An Adventurous Missionary Teacher Finds a Home in a New Culture

To be born at the farthest point north in the British Isles—at John O'Groats—is a distinction. The village, a tiny, isolated community, survives because of a hotel, a herring fleet, the ferry line to the Orkneys, and the families of the officers who maintain the lighthouse. The name of the town comes from a Dutchman, Jan de Groot, who came to Scotland in the time of James IV. A public record lists twenty-eight owners with the name "Groot" from 1496 to 1741.

One of the Groots built an octagonal house with eight doors and an eight-sided table, enabling each member of the family to take the head of the table, thus preventing quarrels over precedence. Imagine a young girl growing up surrounded by a story like this and listening to the steady beat of the waves on the lighthouse seawall.

Margaret Henderson was from old Scottish stock. The Hendersons were scattered across the landscape of the Highlands, including those who fought in the Glencoe battle in 1346 and the reformer Alexander Henderson of Fifeshire, and some even claimed to be related to the Lords of the Isles. Since the early 1500s, Henderson families have lived in Caithness. This lonely corner of Great Britain was truly home to Margaret.

The world of the youth of John O'Groats was, however, much larger. Soldiers of the Caithness Fencibles had gone to suppress the Irish Rebellion, and others died in the Peninsular War while storming the gates of Salamanca and Burgos. News from the far corners of the world filtered through to Caithness by way of soldiers, sailors, and merchants. Margaret grew up with much information about the world because she lived near a major port of a seafaring people.

Both bitter and sweet memories interlaced the fabric of her growing up in that lonely corner of Scotland. There was the tragic wreck of the ferry, caught in a sudden storm that swept in like a fierce animal on the prowl. In that violent event, a beloved school chum was lost with a dozen more neighbors. It was a sad day when they laid her friend's slight body to rest in a tiny plot near the lighthouse—no fence, no gate, just a lonely cross formed by two broken oars wedged into cracks in the rocky soil.

Margaret learned early about life's quick movement between joy and sorrow. The words of the Gospel hymn "Jesus, Savior, Pilot Me" were sure promises for those who faced "hiding rocks and treacherous shoals." The steady beat of the waves on the lighthouse seawall was a daily reminder that life is a stormy voyage over uncharted seas.

Her middle name, "Sinclair," came from her mother's side of the family. It was a time-honored tradition in Scottish families that the mother's maiden name be carried on by the eldest daughter. Her birth name, "Margaret," has been a popular name for Scottish girls for centuries. She had a grandmother and two great-aunts on both the Sinclair and Henderson sides with that name. But she did not like being called "Maggie." She was always to be known as "Margaret."

She was taught to be straitlaced, which literally meant that she always tightened the laces of her bodice so that not even a hint of her graceful expanding breasts would be exposed to peering eyes. Strict rules guided relations between young men and women. This separation was clearly emphasized in the seating in church services. Men sat on one side of the sanctuary, and women, on the other.

The Holy Scriptures made all this very clear: male and female were created as such by God for a divine purpose. Boys and girls were expected to be chaste in all their ways. Words like "intercourse" and "sexual pleasure"—and certainly "cohabitation"—were stricken from their vocabulary. Boys and girls would never dare use fingers or hands to describe the intimate marital acts. The verses from the Epistles of John and Peter were often quoted: "Temptation roams around like both a shining angel and a roaring lion. . . . Flee from the devil and he will depart from you." The lifting of the skirt or a reference to the lump in the crotch were signs of gross perversion. Sex education was as far from the minds of parents as the poles of north and south.

Margaret was a daughter of a strict United Presbyterian family. She never dreamed of any other life. The Hendersons were members of the United Presbyterian Church, a psalm-singing denomination that had separated from the Church of Scotland in the 1840s. This new church had resolved to receive no funds from the church tax allotment but to support their congregations by freewill offerings. They used no musical instruments in their worship. It was bare-bones religion. The denomination believed strongly in an educated clergy and laity. Margaret's grandfather John Henderson had attended the Tain Academy. Her father was the factor for several estates in and around Wick and traveled to Edinburgh each year by coastal steamer to transact business for the lairds he served.

"Margaret, now that you're nearing the end of primary school, what are you going to do?" asked her father.

"Father, I think I want to be a teacher. I really like children," replied Margaret. "But first I have to go to secondary school and then the normal school. But the schools are in Wick and Inverness, says my teacher."

"My dear, perhaps you could stay with my cousin Martha on Harbour Place in Wick and attend the secondary school there. You could help her in the small eating place she keeps. Let's speak with her after church this Sunday," offered her father.

Margaret was able to live with her father's cousin for four years while she attended secondary school. It was only ten miles from home, so she would go home on holidays and saw her family every Sunday at church services. She and her schoolmates would sometimes take their lunches down to the harbor and watch the ships come and go. The teenage girls also kept their eyes peeled for glimpses of handsome sailors on shore leave.

The only famous person she ever saw as she was growing up was a son of the Stevenson family, Robert Louis, who had written a book called *Treasure Island*. His father was the government inspector of lighthouses along the rugged coast of northern Scotland. The family lived in a granite "big house" down by the harbor. She remembered reading that he died as a young man of forty-four from tuberculosis.

The small congregation in Wick belonged to a very missionary-minded church. Their denomination supported missions in Abyssinia, Egypt, and India. Margaret was very impressed when she heard Miss MacNab, a missionary teacher from the Punjab, speak at their church about the spiritual and material needs of the people of that far-off nation. Margaret thought, "Could I ever be a missionary teacher like her?"

"Father, do you think that the mission board would ever accept someone young and inexperienced like me?" Margaret asked. "Maybe I am too young, but I would really like to write to Edinburgh to see if there might be a place for me overseas."

"Daughter Margaret, my firstborn, it would be very hard for your mother and me to see you go so far away for so long," her father replied. "Yet when we dedicated you to the Lord the day of your baptism, we pledged to let God's will be done in your life. Perhaps this is the way that God wants you to go. Why should we say no to a call that seems to come from God? Listen carefully to what God is saying to you, my dear one."

Shortly after her twenty-first birthday, a letter came from Edinburgh asking her to travel there for an interview with the board secretary for India. Her proud parents and younger siblings saw her off at the Wick train station for her first adventure away from home.

A few months later, Margaret was informed that she was accepted for a teaching post in the School for Expatriate Children in Lahore, India. The commissioning was set for Reformation Sunday, October 31, 1901, at the Presbytery of the Highlands in Wick. She would serve as a probationary missionary teacher for five years under the care of the Presbytery of the Punjab.

Six months later, she sailed from the Port of Glasgow on the SS *Imperial,* bound for Bombay via the Suez Canal. Two old family trunks, stuffed with her clothes, books, and medicines for subtropical living, were stored in the ship's hold.

Onboard ship, she found herself among an assortment of individuals and families who were traveling east for many reasons. They were soldiers, merchants, consular officials, and missionaries. A young consular officer took a particular interest in Margaret and sought out her attention on the deck and in the library and dining room. She tried to be distant and reserved, but to no avail.

"Hey, young lady, how about joining us for a game of quoits on the upper deck this afternoon?" called out Jock MacCowan.

"Sorry, sir, but I can't even toss a ball across a bum," she jauntily replied.

"Well, at least you could stop by and watch a game," he returned.

But that was about all the response he could elicit from Margaret. She was not interested in the young men. Her thoughts were caught up only in the missionary dream of service to her Lord among the unconverted in the land to which God had called her.

The steamer of the Anglo-India Line sailed every three months between Glasgow and Port Alexandria, and another ship took the passengers from a Red Sea port to Bombay. The ocean voyage took nearly two months, which included a week in Cairo, where she stayed with missionaries. For a young woman the voyage was an exciting adventure into a strange new world.

She was met at the Port of Bombay by a senior missionary couple who took her by train to Lahore. There, she began a year of language study with another single missionary and a young couple from Paisley who had arrived a few weeks before.

Margaret's arrival was in the desperate month of June, with unbearable 115-degree temperatures. She suffered from heat rash during the first months—not the prickly heat familiar to most British during the summer months but a deep and scalding itch that crawled, day by day, from her shoulders to her armpits to the base of her spine, from her groin and up across the belly. Along with these irritations, she was beset with dysentery, with headaches, rumblings, and twisting in the belly. There were also the midsummer visitations of malaria.

Early in her first year, she learned to keep busy, if only to preserve her sanity. When the canal bank roads were open, she rode horseback with a native evangelist to attend church services in the villages. When the monsoon churned rural trails into quagmires, she accompanied the house boy on his trips to the market and up and down the narrow streets of the Bhera bazaar, listening to the chatter of the shopkeepers and laborers. The trouble with that activity was that it brought sweat and further irritated her raw flesh. Always lay ahead of her the steaming nights when she tried to sleep.

By the first week in August, the monsoon season reached its parboiling peak. The days began with sunshine, and the temperature rose to over ninety degrees by seven o'clock. At ten, the first curtains of rain drew steam from walks and roofs. Again at three, the rain returned, pulling vapor from the soaked soil. By five o'clock, the moisture-laden air was hot once more, and the evening pour began. But she saw that her companions were bearing up without much complaining. Perhaps she could make it, too.

In addition to her language classes, there were cultural

orientation classes taught by both Punjabi and expatriate teachers. She was introduced to the major religions of the Punjab
Province, among them Sikhism, a major religion of the region.
It was a progressive faith, well ahead of its time, when it was
founded five hundred years before. It had a following of about
twenty-three million, the majority living in the Punjab province. Sikhism proclaimed a gospel of devotion and remem-
brance of God at all times, emphasized truthful living and the
equality of mankind, and denounced superstitions and blind
rituals.

The mission school was founded to serve the children
of the foreign missionaries, the families of the British Colonial Service, and other children from British-Punjabi families.
The Anglican chaplain to the British garrison was assigned to
teach the religion classes, and Margaret taught English gram-
mar and British literature.

The small Christian community met for divine worship
and Sunday school each Sabbath in the assembly hall of the
school building.

The Bahadur Singh family was one of the prominent
Sikh families of the city who sent their children to the mission
school. As the Sikh religion was more open to Christianity
than were either the Hindu or Muslim faiths, the Sikhs were
not concerned that their children's faith would be harmed by
some Christian teaching, and of course, they would learn English well in their studies.

This family included an eighteen-year-old boy, Amir,
who was an excellent student. He had indicated in the graduation yearbook that he intended to study law the following

fall. He was tall and handsome and seemed mature beyond his years.

Now that Amir was no longer a student in Margaret's class, she felt that perhaps she could be helpful to him as he prepared for the law school entrance examinations. These exams were very rigorous and designed to admit only the best students to the coveted fifty places in the first-year class.

Margaret drew Amir aside after the graduation program and said, "Amir, let me congratulate you on winning the Mackay Prize. Let me know if you need any special help as you prepare for the law school entrance exams."

Often after school hours, Amir would stop by her classroom to say hello but also to bring a draft of an essay for her criticism. Margaret was drawn not only to his brilliance but also to his stately demeanor and soft-spoken speech.

Margaret could not but feel attracted to him. Amir was certainly eyeing his teacher with more than casual glances. While she lectured on verb tenses, he was enthralled by the image of her lithe body set against the lush tropical flora outside the window. It was like a vision of the Garden of Eden.

He thought, "Oh, Satan, don't put those ideas in my head—that woman is tempting me to imagine what is behind the fig leaf! How lovely her smooth, white skin, her brownish red hair, and her well-formed breasts."

More than once he caught himself day dreaming in her class.

She also found herself waking up in the morning with his name on her lips. She would stay up late reading a history of the English language, then turn off the lights, and roll and twist in bed. She would pull the blankets over her head and want to see him, talk to him, and hear him laugh. She thought about the cycle of desire. Can this be a dream? Is this really love?

One evening, he stopped by her apartment, bringing with him a paper for her criticism and improvement. This was a daring step for him. He cautiously knocked on her door.

"Why, Amir, what a surprise. Come in. It is good to see you. Would you like some coffee? Tea? How was your first week of classes?"

"Well, miss, I thought that I knew English better than I really do. I got my first exam back with a note: 'Good content but poor sentence structure.' Teacher, I really need some help. Can you look over this rewrite of the paper? I need to hand it in next Monday."

This visit was the first of other calls for help. Margaret responded with enthusiasm to each request from "a favorite pupil." Amir's visits to her lodgings became more frequent. She could nearly set her watch by his knock at the door, usually around eight in the evening. Moti, the cook, had gone home. Amir and Margaret would huddle together around the round table of the dining room.

Amir stayed later and later each evening. Margaret enjoyed his company. She would walk slowly with him to the door, take his hand to say good-bye, and only reluctantly let his hand go. At times she would let her fingers slowly touch the back of his hands as they parted.

The magic power of sexual attraction seemed to shower over them.

One evening, he simply said, "Miss, can I stay a little longer since I really don't want to leave you alone?"

Margaret showed no reluctance and sat down beside him and started to take up his next day's lesson. He moved closer to her and put his arm around her slender waist.

"Miss," he said in a small, tight voice. "I can't go on like this."

Margaret replied, "Neither can I. But if we keep seeing each other like this every other night, the older missionaries will probably send me back to Scotland on the next boat."

"Listen, miss," he spoke louder. "Listen, just listen." His gaze was frozen on the cuff of his coat. "I love you."

"No, no," she replied and took his hand. They were both trembling. Margaret blurted out: "Amir, I have been in love with you since I don't know when. I tried not to be, but I am very much in love with you."

Amir nodded and squeezed her hand. "But there's no place for us to go. We can't have a real relationship!"

"We already have a relationship, but it can't go beyond this. I mean, people just can't keep seeing us together so often."

"Oh, I know that. Miss, it's up to you, whatever you say."

"But don't you care that I am a teacher and you are a sort of special student? And I am a foreigner? Don't you care what the mission will think? It seems crazy, but I really do love you."

Amir held Margaret close. "Of course I care deeply about you. I wish you were the shopkeeper's down the road, but you are not!"

Margaret knew that this relationship was risky and perhaps it would never work out and that she might live to regret it. Yet she also thought, "I am tired of pretending and fighting with myself. Deep down in my heart, I want Amir and I can never give him up."

Amir also knew that he might lose the newly found love of his life. He desperately wanted her as his own.

"But there's one thing more, Amir," Margaret said, pulling herself up straight. "You can no longer call me 'miss.' It must be Margaret from now on."

The relationship was now more than that of friends. Margaret wanted Amir enough to go to the mission, ask to be released from her commitment, and marry her Punjabi sweetheart.

Margaret had been in the Punjab now for nearly two years and had observed the faithful practice of many school children of the Sikh religion. She knew there were differences within this religious community—some were more orthodox than others. But all Sikhs seemed to be more progressive than the Hindu majority.

"Margaret, I know you are a Christian. We Sikhs have much in common with you. We, too, try to remember God at all moments in our daily life. We, too, believe like Christians in the equality of every person before God. We often recite a teaching of Nanak Dev, our founder: 'There is no Hindu. There is no Muslim.'"

"Amir, from what I know about your religion, you are not superstitious and talk a lot about truthful living. Just what do you mean?" asked Margaret.

"It means simply that we should live out what we believe," answered Amir. "I remember hearing a verse in a devotional

service in school that went something like this: 'Jesus said, I am
the way, the truth and the life.' Is that the right verse?"

"Yes, those are just the right words—it is a short verse,
but it says it all. My father would say the same thing in the
advice he gave us as children: 'Now practice what you preach.'"

Amir continued, "We Sikhs do not believe in divorce like
you Christians, even though at times that is the only way out
of a failed marriage. I believe that Jesus recognized that at times
divorce might be necessary. In the Sikh marriage service, the
final words are, 'Now two bodies will become a single soul.'"

Margaret replied, "You know that Jesus said something
like that. 'And the two shall be one flesh.'"

Amir turned to another subject about which they spoke
often—remembering God at all times. "Margaret, you and I
have talked often about feeling the presence of God wherever
we are at any time of day or night. We Sikhs believe that God
can be seen everywhere with the inward eye and in the heart."

Margaret and Amir talked about the gender of God, which
was a very important belief of the Sikhs. For them God had no
gender. Margaret read to him the passage from one of the Gos-
pels that told about Jesus' weeping over Jerusalem: "O Jerusalem, how often I would have gathered you under my wing, as a
hen protects her little ones, but you would not."

Margaret felt that Amir was a Christian in his heart. She
was challenged by Amir's complete commitment to the Sikh
religion, yet he always seemed open and curious to learn more
about Christianity. He was neither afraid of hell nor enticed
by heaven. He said simply that the final destiny of all God's
creatures is a spiritual union with God, which is the only real

salvation. Margaret was comfortable to be in love with such a wonderful human being who lived every hour remembering God's power and goodness.

As the school year unfolded, there were long and stern conversations with the elder missionaries and yet some more encouraging words from a younger married couple in the mission. The older missionaries laid before her the problems that she would have as a foreigner who marries into a Punjabi family. Their children would grow caught up in the tensions of two cultures. Did she really want to cut herself off from her native roots and put down new roots in a foreign soil?

More than once an older woman, Mrs. Dalrymple, warned her about the frequent visit of the young Punjabi law student to her living quarters. Of course, she probably forgot her own courting trysts behind the barn and in the hay long years ago!

"My dear," said her elder colleague, "I have a growing concern about your living alone. You may be tempting providence and not realize the dangers of being alone so often with a male student. And if you marry into a Punjabi family, do you realize how restrictive your life will become?"

But there was the younger couple, the McIntires, who were sympathetic. They had read an article in the *Missionary Messenger* about an American Presbyterian missionary in Japan who had married a woman of that country. The mission on the field had ruled that she was no longer eligible to serve as a member of the mission but could only be listed as a wife of a missionary. The case was then appealed by the husband to the mission board in New York, which overruled the Japan mission. Rory and Fiona McIntire were convinced that the practice of

Christian liberty was at stake in this case and each missionary should be free to enter the matrimonial relationship to which God guides them.

Amir and Margaret were married the next spring—she was twenty-three, and he was twenty and a second-year law student. They had two separate marriage ceremonies, according to the Sikh and Christian traditions. The Sikh ceremony *(anand karaj)* was performed in the company of the guru Grantha Sahib, around whom the couple circled four times. After the ceremony the couple was then considered "a single soul in two bodies," as the guru informed them in his closing words.

The Christian marriage service was preformed by the Anglican chaplain. Margaret wore a simple white dress with a Henderson tartan scarf. Since the Sikh religion is not a proselytizing faith, converts to Sikhism were welcomed, but Christians were not obligated to leave their religion if they married a Sikh. Amir and Margaret simply said to their friends and family that they were so much in love with each other that it never occurred to either of them to try to convert the other.

Amir was faithful to the five *K*s of the Sikh religion: uncut hair, a small comb, a circular heavy metal bracelet, the ceremonial short sword, and the *kaccha,* a special undergarment. The five *K*s were considered to have both practical and symbolic purposes.

The newly married couple moved into his parental home in Lahore. Margaret quietly resigned from the mission but continued to teach her classes. Life went on without a ripple. The words of the Scottish poet in "The Pipes of Lucknow" soon became embedded in Punjabi–Pakistani history: "The tartan clove the turban as the Gumpti cleaves the plain."

In July 1920, Amir Bahadur Singh was appointed by the viceroy of India to the position of chief justice of the supreme court of the Punjab province. He was now to be addressed as His Honor, Doctor Amir Bahadur Singh.

Two women—his wife, Margaret, and their daughter, Elizabeth, had come to his office to wait for him to finish the judicial deliberations of the day. Margaret, now nearing forty years of age, and sixteen-year-old Elizabeth, a first-year student at the Lahore Women's College, sat in his elegant office.

Elizabeth broke the silence.

"Mother, we had a very interesting visitor at the college today. His name was Mr. Gandhi. He had just come back from South Africa, where he was a labor negotiator. He talked about the seven deadly sins, like politics without principle and wealth without work. He is starting a movement to change things in India that he calls a nonviolent and noncooperative scheme which will give our people freedom from the colonial government. It sounded rather scary. I'd like to get father's opinion about it. Here is the article in the college newspaper."

"Your father is a very wise man," Margaret replied. "I am sure he will give you some guidance."

Margaret impatiently waited for His Honor and lifted up a stone paperweight from the top of the huge mahogany desk.

"Elizabeth, this is a piece of flagstone that I brought with me from Caithness long years ago. That is the part of Scotland where I grew up. Our family has few souvenirs that came with me from the old country in 1902. This piece of flagstone was given to me by my father when I left for India. He told me that it would always remind me of my native soil."

"This piece of stone is really important to you?" Margaret asked.

"Dear, yes it is important. This stone takes on a fine polish and is used for the floors of cathedrals, roofs, garden walls, and even the work surfaces in the kitchen. It is exported all over the world—something like we Scots who are scattered to the far corners of the British Empire. Scotland is a poor country, except for our people. Thomas Carlyle once said that 'the principal export of Scotland is people.'"

I also recall a poem by Robert Burns that I learned as a child: "From scenes like these, old Scotia's grandeur springs / That makes her lov'd at home, rever'd abroad: / Princes and lords are but the breath of kings, / 'An honest man's the noblest work of God' . . . " (from "The Cotter's Saturday Night").

## 8 | The Story of a Texas Cowboy and Indian Fighter

*This story is largely based on an oral interview in 1936 by Ruby Mosley, San Angelo, Texas. The original text is on file in the manuscript collection* American Life Histories: Manuscripts from the Federal Writers' Project, 1936–1940. *This collection numbers approximately 300,000 items. In the introduction to this collection appears the following description of the project: "The plight of the unemployed writer, and indeed of anyone who could qualify as a writer such as a teacher, lawyer, or a librarian, during the years of the Great Depression, was a concern not only to the Roosevelt Administration, but also to writers' organizations and persons of liberal and academic persuasions. It was felt, generally, that the New Deal could come up with appropriate work conditions for this group other than blue collar jobs on construction projects."[1]*

Daniel Boone Sinclair, Jr., was born in 1863 in Madison County, Missouri. His father, Daniel Boone Sinclair, Sr., was killed when his son was young, and his mother died shortly thereafter. Her name was Melvina Graham Sinclair. He was one of several orphaned children. He left for Texas with a group of neighbors when he was eleven years of age. There he was adopted by Mr. and Mrs. J. A. Goodnight, who owned the Half Circle Box Ranch "just north of the Pease River" in the Panhandle near the present-day towns of Childress and Vernon, Texas.

He lived with them for sixteen years and said, "They were the only parents I really ever knew." They gave him a practical, moral, and religious formation. They displayed photos of all their children at different times being baptized. The old-fashioned baptisms were held at the river, where hundreds of people would gather.

Daniel's first marriage was to Leila Fields Sinclair. They had three children. She died at an early age. His second marriage was to Lillie Cain, a quarter-blood Comanche Indian, to which J. A., J. D., and Lillie Sinclair Mullinax were born. As an Indian fighter, he told many stories.

"Daniel, tell me about the rescue of that sixteen-year-old Millie MacDonald who was kidnapped by the Indians," asked his sidekick, Will.

"Well, partner, that was when the Texas Rangers sent me to try to get the girl back after all the MacDonald family except Millie were murdered. They were one of the wealthiest families in those parts."

"Well, did you get her? How did you pull that one off?"

"Me and my buddy traveled through the snow until we saw the light of their campfires. We just snuck up and waited until they were well asleep before we got Millie, stole one of their ponies for her, and gave her an extra gun. Yeah, we got her out alive, and she lived to be a grand old lady. I tell you, them early Texas women settlers were tough!"

The next tale is too far-out to believe, but the following was what Daniel Boone Sinclair, Jr., told the interviewer:

Two years later the Indians were still seeking revenge. They returned and captured twelve men and carried them to Red Canyon as captives. They chose Charlie

Smith first and gave him due course of punishment and in turn gave each what they thought would be his punishment. There was nothing too bad for those heartless creatures to do. Poor Charlie, they hanged him to a tree and skinned him alive, taking his finger and toe nails to make the hide complete for display. As they were completing the torture, eleven rangers and I appeared on the scene.

We really scattered the Indians and killed several but they carried away their dead with them, also Charlie's hide. The Indians thought Charlie was dead and so did we, and went on with the skirmish which lasted 'most all night. The citizens were released and sent back home. Mrs. Fad Eskew had a nightmare that night and tried to get Mr. Eskew to go help Charlie. He only said, "Go back to sleep. It's too late to help Charlie now, he is dead." She went to sleep and the dream was repeated. This time she said, "Fad, go get a bunch of men and help Charlie, if you don't I will."

This time Mr. Eskew rounded up a gang of men, rode out well armed to do what they could. Charlie was gone and they searched around and found him. He had obtained his own freedom and was trying to make it to Fort Griffith. They picked him up and rushed him to the fort to give him treatment. Of course it took many days for him to recover and grow a new skin. Charlie lived eleven years and fourteen days after the disaster.

Mr. Sinclair was appointed an agent of the federal government in his later years.

The Comanche Indians were put on the reservation. Imagine the anger of the Comanche tribe, which had once roamed freely over 60,000 square miles after the Treaty of Medicine Lodge (1867), to be placed on a reservation of less than 5,000 square miles. In 1892 the government negotiated the Jerome Agreement, further reducing their reservation to 480,000 acres, with an allotment of only 160 acres per person. The era of the Comanche dominance had come to an end on the frontier.

Daniel Boone Sinclair got involved in some crooked deals as an agent of the federal government's Bureau of Indian Affairs. The tribes had been placed on a reservation in what is today Oklahoma, near Lawton. In the treaty of 1882 between the government and the Comanche, Kiowa, and Apache tribes, the government assumed the responsibility "to furnish 4,000 beeves for their meat supply each year," according to Mr. Sinclair's interview. In the last paragraph of that interview, Mr. Sinclair stated clearly, "I went up and issued the meat as it was needed." As an agent of the U.S. government, he was free to allocate the meat promised to the Indians at his own discretion. Thus he became a rather dark character in his dealings and made a career of exploiting the Native Americans and their reservation lands.

Was there any oversight of his duties? Probably not. Little by little, he acquired a number of head of cattle by keeping for himself some of the cattle destined for the tribe. He then set up his own company, D. B. S. Cattle, with the special Half Circle Box brand of his herd cattle.

Since his second wife, Lillie Cain, was one-quarter Comanche, he claimed falsely that he had "Indian blood." Thus, he attended the annual powwow on the reservation with his mixed-blood daughter, Lillie Sinclair Mullinax. He learned to speak enough "Indian" so that he was seen at least as a friend of the tribe, even though not a member.

By the early 1900s, Daniel Boone Sinclair was known as a prosperous cattle dealer. He had acquired a section of land at the edge of the reservation through a clause in the treaty that left some marginal land for purchase by white settlers. Since he was intimately aware of the conditions of some of the Indian families who were not using their land, he also brokered some deals with white families to acquire tracts of "Indian lands." Some Indians had little or no interest in becoming farmers since their traditions were related to hunting, not farming.

By the early twentieth century, Mr. Sinclair, now past fifty, was comfortably settled in his own ranch with his wife and their three children. He was no longer "a wandering orphan boy," but he had made it as a prosperous rancher. The details of the ways he had acquired his wealth were hidden in the falsified documents of the actual number "of the 4,000 beeves" he had turned over to the reservation for slaughter each year and the amount of the payments he had made to several Indian families who sold him their reservation plots. Perhaps these documents might be unearthed in some dark corner of the archives of the Bureau of Indian Affairs and confirm this story.

Years later at the annual powwow on the Comanche Reservation in Oklahoma, J. P. Sinclair, Daniel's great-grand-son, and J. A. Parker, the great grandson of Chief Quanah

Parker, strolled through the Comanche Museum together. They stood looking at some old black-and-white photos taken in the 1890s. One picture was of Chief Quanah Parker and a white man in cowboy garb.

"Why that's the old man himself," said J. P. Sinclair. "That's my great-grandpa. Yeah, the caption reads 'Chief Quanah Parker with D. B. Sinclair, Jr., Federal Land Agent.'"

"My great-grandpa was a close friend of old Daniel," J. A. Parker replied. "There are a lot of stories about the two of them making some shady deals with land and cattle. I wouldn't be surprised if at least half of those stories are true."

The author at the gate to El Cementerio de Disidentes,
Valparaíso, Chile, 2005

A watercolor of Iona Abbey by cousin Freddie Mill

"Margaret" Sinclair and cousin Ian Sinclair at the ruins of Castle
Sinclair-Girnigoe, Noss Head, Caithness

Rev. Alexander G. Mill and daughter, Barbara, Cambridge,
England, c. 1960

The author and sister, Catherine Grace, at the old stone croft,
Achavarigil, Calder, near Halkirk, Caithness

The ruins of the ancient castle of the Sinclairs of the Isles, Noss
Head, Caithness

# 9 | The Stonemason and the Psychologist

## The Stonemason

This is the story of a stonemason who carved out a new life on the Canadian frontier and his granddaughter who became a pioneer in the evaluation of juvenile delinquents. Their lives in the New World encompassed the years from 1881 to 1977.

William, son of Henderson Sinclair and Margaret Nicolson, was the eldest grandson of the family that had been cleared from the Halkirk farm to Wick in the early 1800s. He was born in 1854.

The tradition of the family was to work as joiners, who crafted plow handles, scythes, sickles, and wagon beds and tongues for farmers. The move to the port city forced them, however, to change their vocation from working with wood to building with stone. Henderson and his sons took up stonemasonry. They found work with the construction crews who were continually repairing the harbor walls and piers, battered by the stiff Arctic blasts that swept in off the rugged North Sea. William's travel document read "occupation—stonemason."

The herring industry was in a slump in the 1870s, and many workers were laid off. William, at age twenty-six, was now engaged to be married to his childhood sweetheart, Isabella Jack, of nearby Skarferry. She was twenty-one and the daughter of a master mariner. Together, they were prepared to face an uncertain future and immigrate to Western Canada.

A notice on the post office bulletin board read: "Free land and a team of horses offered to settlers by the Manitoba

Immigration Office. Apply at the desk." Some of their relatives had already gone to Canada a few years before, so they were not totally ignorant of the challenges and dangers of going out to the Canadian frontier.

The day after their marriage in her uncle's home in Inverness, they boarded a train for the Port of Glasgow and embarked on the SS *Hanoverian* for Canada. It was a rough crossing of three long weeks before docking at Montreal.

They arrived in Montreal in baking heat, which in those days without air conditioning was insufferable amid the closeness of the grain elevators and wharfs. Gone were the sea breezes and the pleasant anesthesia of shipboard routine.

After Montreal, they spent three days riding by train to Winnipeg, where they spent a few days before moving on the recently completed extension of the Canadian Pacific Railway to Portage La Prairie.

The land agent who met them at the train station directed them to Township No. 11, Range XXII—West, six miles south of Bradwardine. The journey was in a wagon over the recently opened dirt track. It was a strange new land of seemingly endless prairies. The tract of land allocated to William was 165.8 acres according to the original land title, which described the homestead as:

> A tract of land whose northern part is broken by a
> deep ravine: in the middle is a level flat, about one
> mile in width: and a southern part which is a broken,
> stony prairie. The soil is very good, being a black loam,
> especially on the flat level, where it is deep and rich. It

is well watered, nearly all the ravines containing water from springs and swamps. There is some good poplar in the western sections, and some elm, oak and ash on the banks of the Assiniboine River which flows through the southeast corner of the township.[1]

Land title of William Sinclair, Bradwardine, Manitoba, 1881

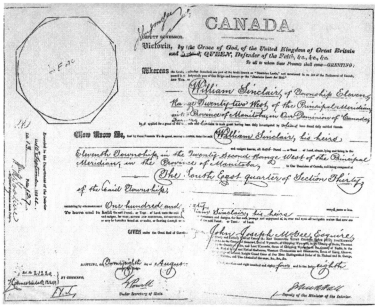

It was a totally new land for the young couple. Within a few months, before the first snows fell in early October, they had built a small log cabin and a barn with a stall for the horses. A load of baled hay and some bags of barley were turned over to them to feed the horses during the long winter. But after that, the land agent told them that they were on their own. Fortunately, two other families were homesteading in the same township, so they were part of a tiny but cohesive immigrant community. William was able to get an eight-hundred-dollar loan from the local bank to buy construction materials, as well as sugar, flour, tea, and salt to see them through the winter.

The winter months at that latitude were long and dreary. Even though they had seen some snow in Northern Scotland, they were not prepared for blizzards that left three feet of it and winds whose blasts penetrated the loose boards of the cabin walls. Only with cups of hot tea, warm underwear, and a dose of Scottish "durness" were they able to survive.

Little did William know the discipline of waiting through the long winter for the first sprigs of green to show amid the receding snow cover. But at last a prairie spring arrived and was met with unbridled joy. He knew little to nothing about handling horses, much less how to hitch them to the plow with a double tree, but with the help of his neighbors, he was able to plow the ground and plant the wheat.

One can hardly imagine a more disastrous event for this young couple: ten acres of wheat ready to be harvested in August wiped out in a short hour by a prairie fire—started how or by whom, nobody knew! Isabella was pregnant with their first child, and their small log cabin sat amid the charred field.

They thought, "Why did we ever leave Scotland?"

A distant cousin of William took them in and found work for him as a bricklayer in Winnipeg. Their second year in Canada was brightened only by the birth of a healthy baby boy, David Alexander, in the spring of 1883. A growing Scottish community in Winnipeg gave the little family both moral and material support as they put down roots in this strange but promising land.

The William Sinclairs prospered in the 1890s as William worked as a bricklayer on several new houses. He earned enough to purchase a building lot in a new housing development in West Winnipeg and later formed his own construction company. As a member of the Masonic Order, he developed contacts in the community and prospered both culturally and financially. The family had moved up to middle-class status.

But tragedy devastated the family in 1908 with William's sudden death. He had taken a contract with the Canadian Pacific Railway to build brick abutments for bridges on the main track in British Colombia. He fell to his death while supervising a bridge in construction near Field, British Colombia. He was the first of his family to be buried in the Westwood Cemetery in Winnipeg.

At the age of twenty-four, David Sinclair fell heir to his father's construction business. He had worked as an apprentice bricklayer but never dreamed that at such an early age he would become the head of the company.

The Sinclairs came to know rather well the new Swedish neighbors who lived down the block. They were the Thoren family, who had changed their name to Turner. They had three

teenage daughters and a younger son. David was attracted to seventeen-year-old Marie Teresa, known as Matilde. Around 1910,
a romance between David and Matilde became serious, and a
wedding date was set for early May 1911. The wedding was
attended by a few relatives from Caithness, including John Peat
Sinclair, who was a theological student at nearby Brandon College. This was the first wedding of our branch of the Sinclairs in
the New World. It was also a union of families that bridged two
countries across the North Sea: Scotland and Sweden.

To this young couple was born a baby girl, Eileen Marie,
known always as Eileen. David did well in the construction
business, as his father had done. He was no longer the son of a
poor immigrant. He also joined the Masonic Order and became
a highly respected member of the community.

## The Psychologist

After World War I, a wave of European immigrants swelled the
worker suburbs of Winnipeg. A progressive provincial government did not hesitate to found a university. By 1924, it had a
department of applied psychology, even though this academic
discipline had only been in existence for a few decades.

Eileen Sinclair chose this field of study and was destined
to became a pioneer in the field of criminology. At this time
university careers were the exception for women, even in progressive Western Canada. Later in her career, Eileen made a
monumental contribution to the field of penal law related to
the pretrial evaluation of juvenile delinquents.

On the other side of the world, in New Zealand, another
young Scot, Paul Ross MacDonald, had chosen a similar field

of study at the University of Dunedin, which had been recently founded in 1900. Paul's family had Scottish roots, and his mother, Sara McClintock MacDonald, was distantly related to George Sinclair of Keiss, Caithness, Scotland, who had come to New Zealand by way of Australia in the previous century.

In the 1880s another migration of Scots was taking place Down Under. The Free Church of Scotland sponsored a carefully planned immigration scheme in New Zealand. Forward-looking pastors and lay leaders in Scotland envisioned the establishment of a New Jerusalem in that far-off corner of the world. The climate was not much different from Scotland, with plenty of rain, and it had fishing, open land for sheep grazing, good timber, and a stable colonial government.

A new university was founded in 1900, the University of Dunedin. One of the students in the applied psychology department was Paul MacDonald. His family had settled near Dunedin, where they have developed a sheep farm. Paul was the great-grandson of George Sinclair of Keiss, Caithness, and his wife, Patty Anderson Sinclair, who had come to New Zealand by way of Australia in the 1840s. Their daughter had married a Ross MacDonald who was a staunch Presbyterian from the Western Isles of Scotland. Paul Ross MacDonald's story is linked to Eileen Marie Sinclair's of Winnipeg, Canada.

The new University of Dunedin needed to send its best students abroad for graduate work so that they could later join the teaching faculty. Paul was recognized early in his career as material for a teaching career. By the early 1930s, he was in line to receive a scholarship with the understanding that he would return and serve on the faculty for at least five years. At the age of twenty-four, Paul won the Balfour Scholarship and was soon off to the far-eastern shore of the North Pacific Ocean and the University of California at Berkeley.

Strong ties between the United States and New Zealand already existed early in the twentieth century. The new nation was located an equal distance from San Francisco and London. New Zealand wanted to explore new connections with the entire world. It was not surprising that the academic committee suggested that Paul MacDonald do graduate work in the United States. The institution at Berkeley was known around the world as a top-flight institution. A new graduate school of social science had been opened in 1928.

For Paul, everything was just right: the climate, the bustle of a big city, the cosmopolitan character of the citizens, and the same feel of the vast Pacific Ocean—but from the other side of the world. He brought with him a special interest in applied psychology as it related to the new penal code that was being debated in the national parliament in Wellington. Many of the islands' original dwellers, the Maori, and the more recent immigrants from the South Pacific islands were seeking employment and a better life in the urban centers of New Zealand. They had trouble integrating into the urban environment, however, which challenged the social services agencies.

Much of the same was true for Eileen as she arrived that same year from Winnipeg. She had won a scholarship that funded most of her studies for a master's degree in psychology. She was left free to chose the particular field of her specialization.

She had grown up in Winnipeg and had experienced the

presence of Native Canadians who moved into the city looking for work and a better life. They suffered cultural alienation
and often experienced police abuse. Many were hauled into
the provincial court and given stiff penalties. But was there
really any careful evaluation of their situation before they were
sent to trial? Eileen began to narrow her focus to this area of
penal law and practice.

One of her professors suggested that she should do her
research on this subject, using the nearby San Quentin Prison
for her fieldwork. A considerable number of minority inmates
were among that prison's population.

She was fortunate to find lodging in International House,
where she got to know students from many different countries.
Paul MacDonald had found lodging there, as well, and he was
also majoring in penal law.

"Hey, MacDonald, can I hitch a ride with you to the
ferry?" called Eileen as she stood on the corner waiting for
the bus.

"Sure, hop in. How did you know my name was Mac-
Donald?" responded Paul.

"That's easy. You're wearing a MacDonald tie," replied
Eileen. "Any Scot can spot the MacDonald tartan!"

"So you're a Scot, too. I know you name is Eileen and
you're from Canada, but what's your last name?"

"Eileen, member of Clan Sinclair, at your orders, Kiwi!"
she jauntily replied.

There were more ferry rides together across the Bay
and many walks together along the wooded paths of the university's campus. They shared stories and experiences about

their families. The MacDonalds had come to New Zealand in the last century from the Western Isles, and the Sinclairs had arrived in Canada a few decades ago from Caithness. They conversed about the old country and the reasons that Scottish people migrated to the far corners of the British Empire.

Soon their conversations turned to more personal subjects, like their plans after they finished their graduate work. Would they be staying longer to do the doctoral program?

"Mac, I am sure going to miss talking to you when I go back to Winnipeg."

"Eileen, you are a very smart and interesting lass. You are really going to make a name for yourself in the field of penal law."

The ferry ride to San Quentin made a routine stop at Battery Park in San Francisco. It was a lovely place to go for a walk and watch the sunset. Paul and Eileen often went there on Saturday afternoons when they returned from a morning of interviews at the prison. The cool breezes from the sea and the luscious growth along the hillside paths lent place, time, and atmosphere for romance.

Two young adults—each in their late twenties—were falling in love by degrees. Both were virgin lovers, experiencing their first real infatuation. The future was uncertain for both. Paul had to return to New Zealand to fulfill his university contract. The war clouds were gathering, and he felt that military service might be thrust upon him when he returned home. Eileen was torn between her love for Paul and her obligations as an only daughter to return to care for her aging parents in Winnipeg.

"Paul, my love, I just can't think of ever leaving you or perhaps even losing you. It's awful to think that you might have to enlist and be sent to fight in that terrible war in Europe—and even be killed!" She broke down in tears and clung tightly to him.

"Eileen, there, there, wipe away those tears, my love. God will take care of me. We will certainly find a way to always be together," he assured her.

They both embraced again and again. Paul's hands dropped down to her waist and found their way below her loose skirt and touched her bare flesh. Eileen relaxed and kissed him on his neck, and they rolled back together on the grass slope.

The sun had set, and they were alone, holding each other in a loving embrace. They could never live without each other. Body and soul were united, and they were one. Darkness was approaching and that made the moment more sublime. Finding complete peace in each other's arms, they felt an unspeakable joy, bound to each other forever.

Mac faced the future with complete honesty. The letters from home and the newspapers told of the long and bitter world conflict that lay ahead of the Allied nations. He did not see how he could escape the military draft when he returned home—single and age twenty-six.

Since New Zealand was surely going to send troops to fight with the British in Europe, he would be drafted when he returned home. The Anzac forces, made up of Australians and New Zealanders, would soon be fighting in the first battles on Europe's southeastern front.

"Eileen, my dearest, don't worry. We'll keep in touch. There's a world penal conference in Honolulu this fall, so perhaps we can see each other in a few months."

"Mac, you are so dear. I can't stand to think what might happen to you."

"Eileen, you really mean 'us.' I can't stand to lose you. Will you marry me?"

"Mac, a hundred times yes, I will marry you. I can never live apart from you."

The days in May moved along quickly as they talked about marriage, now or sometime soon. Eileen would have loved to go with him to New Zealand, but she was the only daughter of aging parents who needed her. Could she ever think of living half way around the world?

Mac would have loved to go with her to Canada, but he was obligated to return to teach for at least five years in New Zealand or repay the twenty thousand dollars of his graduate expenses. Could he find a new career in Canada? Would he be shirking his patriotic duty by leaving New Zealand and thus avoiding the draft?

"See you at the convention in Honolulu in the fall, God willing. Don't forget to write every week," said Paul as they held each other in a long embrace and kissed farewell. Paul slowly walked up the gangplank to sail back to his homeland. Within weeks after his homecoming, a draft notice was in his mailbox instructing him to report for induction at the local army depot in Dunedin.

Boot camp was compressed into six short weeks as the pressing need for fresh troops in the European theater heated up. Within two months, Paul, now Lt. Paul MacDonald of the 77th Anzac Battalion, was at the frontlines in northern Greece.

Weeks later he was reported killed in action in the early days of the campaign to repel the Nazi invaders. A chaplian sent Eileen the following letter:

Dear Ms. Sinclair:

I regret to inform you of the death in combat of your fiancé, Lt. Paul Ross MacDonald. He died during an engagement near Neapolis, Greece, between Anzac troops who were supporting the Greek patriots against the enemy. The date of his death was January 10, 1942, and he was buried there in a military cemetery. He left in my keeping the enclosed letter to be sent to you if he should not survive the conflict.

"Mac," as Paul was known to his comrades, was a noble spirit and generous soul. He often assisted me in the service of Holy Communion and led the hymns at Evensong—sometimes with the bullets flying overhead.

Paul's death occurred on the ancient plain where the ruins of the Roman city of Philippi once stood. It was on that ancient battlefield that the Greek patriots and the Allied troops took their stand at great cost of human life but were able to stop the Nazi invaders and thus save the Greek homeland.

Providence seemed to rule that your Paul's death took place in a struggle to assure freedom for the Greek people. We can not understand God's plan for Paul's short life and much less for all our lives, but we know as a certainty that each of us is always the object of God's love and grace.

Paul left with me the enclosed letter addressed to you and to be sent if he should not survive in combat.

May God comfort you in your sorrow by His Spirit.

Respectfully yours,

Chaplain Ian S. Buchannon


Dearest Eileen,

I have asked Chaplain Buchannon of the 77th Anzac Battalion to send you this letter if I should die in this terrible war.

You are the only one I ever truly loved. I cherished you more than life itself. You saw in me much more than I ever dreamed was there. You were my queen in much more than that of royalty—you were the one I truly honored and adored. God seemed to have meant us for each other.

Even though we were never able to marry, you were truly my soul mate and confidant. In heaven we shall surely meet.

Your adoring lover,

Paul


Among the photos in Eileen's trunk that came to her relatives after her death in 1991 was an unmarked photo of a young soldier. Could this photo have been of Eileen's Paul?

Paul and Eileen had both filed their wills and final testaments.

*From the Registry of Public Documents, Dunedin, New Zealand*

Re: the disposition of the will of Paul Ross MacDonald, deceased, January 10, 1942, near Neapolis, Greece, a junior office of the 77th Anzac Battalion.

I leave my apartment, hunting lodge and all my personal assets to The Trust for Troubled Youth of the City of Dunedin. My personal library is to be donated to the University of Dunedin.

*From the Registrar, Madison, Indiana, United States of America*

Re: the disposition of the will of Eileen Marie Sinclair, retired employee of the Indiana State Correctional System.

I leave all my financial assets to Hanover College as a permanent endowment to establish the Sinclair International Studies Program. My stamp collection is to be given to the son of my second cousin, David Sinclair, who bears the name of my beloved father, David Alexander Sinclair. My personal effects are to be disposed of according to the decision of my executor, John Henderson Sinclair.

In the memorial service held for Dr. Sinclair in the lovely chapel of Hanover College, these words were pronounced: "Here on the high bluff overlooking the Ohio River—this heavily traveled highway of so many immigrant families of North America, it is most fitting that Eileen Marie Sinclair would plant her dream of an international student scholarship fund to help coming generations build a global village of peace, human community, and justice."

Eileen's ashes were placed beside the graves of her parents and grandparents in the family plot in Winnipeg. Among the relatives present for the interment was a young woman, a distant cousin who was recently appointed a professor of psychology at a Manitoba university.

Eileen's ashes were carried from Madison, Indiana, to Winnipeg, Manitoba, by a clergy relative whom she had asked to officiate at her burial. The customs agent at the international border asked the pastor if he had anything to declare as he entered Canada. He hesitated a moment and then replied, "No, sir, nothing to declare. I am only going to visit some cousins in Winnipeg."

In his heart, however, he was thinking, "Yes, I have something to declare to the world: the memory of a beloved relative who drank deeply from the cultures of two sister nations in the North American continent. She was a highly skilled professional who served, without reserve, troubled youth and their families. She was a woman who rose above personal disappointment in her life to leave behind a noble legacy of service to humankind."

## 10 | Henderson Peat Sinclair, Carpenter-Soldier in World War I

### Two Voyages to Canada

Harry's full name was Henderson Peat Sinclair. In fact, all the children of Henderson Sinclair and Martha Peat Sinclair carried their mother's maiden name as their middle name. He was the third generation of Sinclairs to carry the name "Henderson," the family name of his maternal great-grandmother and his father. The Hendersons were an Orcadian family, whereas the Sinclairs were an ancient Caithness family dating in Scotland from the fifteenth century. The Peat family had also lived around Edinburgh at Ratho Station for centuries.

There were eight children in his birth family—Christina, Henderson, Jamesina, John, George, Martha, Willie, and Robert. Daily life for a village family that had settled in the great industrial city of Glasgow in 1899 was difficult. Harry went out to work at the age of fourteen as a carpenter's apprentice. His father was a carpenter, as had been his great-grandfather William. Harry was tall and muscular and quickly learned the basic skills as he observed and assisted the master carpenter. The construction of ships on Clydebank had slowed considerably, as had the building of the new estates around Glasgow, and he spent many days without work. It seemed that it was time to seek work abroad in some corner of the empire.

His uncle William "Tyke" Durrand had left for Western Canada in the early 1900s and wrote about the possibilities for artisans of all trades to find work in the new communities in British Colombia where his family had settled. Harry earned enough money for his passage to Canada, traveled by rail to Revelstoke—a rugged pioneer settlement—and found work. Uncle Tyke had a construction job on the new Canadian Pacific Railway and gave him a place to stay. This was 1907, and the future seemed bright. It was his first great adventure. He dreamed of putting down roots, marrying his sweetheart back in the old country, and returning to build a life on the frontier. After a couple of years there, he could not resist the pull to return to see if Jennie would join him as his life's partner on this adventure. By early 1909, he was back in Glasgow and visited his beloved.

Jennie had fallen in love with another, however, thinking that Harry would not return from British Colombia. On the positive side, his brother John, a theological student in London, had decided to go to Canada to finish his studies since the Bible school in London where he was enrolled was closing for financial reasons. Long discussions were held around the kitchen table of the Henderson Sinclair home on Dunard Street in Glasgow. Would all the family move to Canada? Father and Mother Sinclair confided in their two eldest sons, Harry and John, that, since the death of twenty-three-year-old Jamesina in 1908, they felt that that had to get away to a new place to distance themselves from their grief. Would it be possible for the four of them—and perhaps with their younger brothers—to immigrate to Canada? Cousin David, already settled in Winnipeg and well established in the brick construction business, might sign their emigration guarantee forms.

By mid-1910 a welcoming letter had come back from

Cousin David, and the trunks were being packed. They agreed that Mother Sinclair, Martha, Willie, and Bobbie would to stay behind for six months until Father Sinclair got a job and found a house to rent. Then the rest of the family would travel to Canada.

The four years of Harry's second stay in British Colombia were good years. After he found work, he rented a room in the home of a Scottish widow from Perth named Margaret Leuchers. She had lost her husband at an early age in the Boer War in South Africa and with his death payment had purchased a house in Vancouver. With the income from renting rooms and her widow's pension, she was able to live comfortably. Margaret found conversation about Scotland easy with Harry. She was twenty-five, and Harry was just thirty. It was no surprise to his Canadian relatives when Harry proposed to Margaret in May 1911. A new life began for Harry with a lovely soul mate from his "ain country." Two children, Greta and wee Harry, were born to this happy couple in 1912 and 1914, respectively.

## The Outbreak of World War I

Canada was a loyal nation of the British Empire, and Canadian troops would undoubtedly be engaged on the western front as the war began to take its terrible toll in human life and treasure. Harry was exempted from the first draft because of his age and marital status. With the pressing need for fresh troops and the persistent war propaganda to recruit, however, Harry reluctantly gave in and signed up in 1916. As a carpenter, he hoped that he would be kept in the back lines to build barracks and would not be so likely to be sent to the front. Harry was also in need of medical attention for a chronic back injury and knew he could get free medical attention in the armed forces.

His army unit, the 231st Battalion of the Canadian Expeditionary Force (CEF), was kept in reserve for training in Vancouver for several months. He was able to see his family on weekends. Wee Harry, now two years of age, would don his father's army cap and parade around the house. He felt disappointed when he could march with his Daddy only as far as the gate to the army compound and had to give back his father's cap. He wept bitterly as he clung to his mother's skirt.

On April 10, 1917, Harry finally departed with his unit for England on a troop transport from Montreal. The Canadians were held in reserve for a month on the Salisbury Plain before going over to France. An article appeared in the *Salisbury General Advertizer* showing the attitude of the local press toward the contingent of Canadian soldiers camped on the plain:

> They came across the wider seas and camped in the damp and cold, with the mud about their knees. They came from the young and old, . . . gallant and gay they were, reckless, perhaps and wild. But they came to lend the needed help and a smile for the eyes of a child . . . and nothing could check them, nothing would stay, though the Huns might strive his worst. . . . And their valor was a blessing and glowed like a blessing of God. . . . The year was still young when

they crossed at last the narrowest sea of the Channel.
. . . And we in England, safe apart, bowed stricken
hearts again. We thanked God with a humble heart
for the brothers who sent us men.

On one long weekend leave, he was able to travel to
Scotland to see his wife's relatives in Perth and visit his Aunt
Cristina in Edinburgh.

By the end of May, his unit proceeded to southern
France, where they were put to work constructing barracks
for German prisoners. But the pressure for fresh troops at the
front soon sent his unit forward, now the 72nd Battalion of
the CEF, to the Villers-au-Bois sector.

There, the troops entered the frontlines and woke up
in a dugout to the smell of wet sandbags and stale farts. He
curled his toes inside his wet boots. The damp dirt floor was
littered with a jumble of paper, bottles, and mugs and the
black-boxed field telephone, all lit by a single candle stuck in
a pool of its own grease. A barely perceptible thinness of the
darkness around the gas curtain told the soldiers that it must
be nearly dawn. As they peered over the crumbling parapets,
they viewed lines of trenches with the mouths of other jagged
dugouts.

It was from the mouth his battalion's dugout that Harry
went "over the top" with his squad to attempt to repair the
barbed wire entanglements in front of the trenches. The military record of his death read "killed in action, August 29,
1917."[1] A record compiled by his field commander, an army
buddy, and Chaplain Ian McNeil might have read as follows:

On the night of August 28, 1917, Henderson Peat
Sinclair was mortally wounded. The 72nd Battalion
had just taken over several new trenches. The retiring
company captain seemed to have been careless in the
details of the sector to the new troops, either through
the pressure of the moment or gross neglect. The first
task facing the fresh troops was to send out a squad to
repair the dilapidated trenches and the barbed wire
entanglement in front of the trenches. There was a
partially concealed path which led to No Man's Land
which was known to the Germans who held a position a hundred yards away. This path could be safely
accessed in the dark, but during the day the Germans
kept a machine gun trained on the gap in the hedge
at which they fired a volley if they saw any activity.

The night that Harry's squad was sent out to repair
the wire entanglement it was broad moonlight. The
Canadian's unit was unaware of the danger. Harry led
the squad and was immediately struck down in the
stomach by a volley of machine gun fire. He fell on
his face in full view of his companions behind him.
At the risk of their lives the company commander
and a sergeant rushed him back to the rear. Twenty
minutes afterwards the doctor at the dressing station
put an end to his agony with a large dose of mor-
phine. From that moment Harry ceased—ceased forever—to be Harry. He lingered through the night,
but in the early morning, the Jesuit priest adminis-
tered Extreme Unction as he died.

The commander reported that they brought his body to the village church beside the military cemetery for the burial service. He added to his report these words: "The sun came out and shone brilliantly as we left the service."

Upon hearing of Harry's death, his sister Christina wrote the following to their brother John. The letter is dated October 24, 1917, and sent from 5 Lockend Cottages, Ratho Station.

Dear Brother,

Just received the sad news about poor Harry. What a short time he got in the trenches. Had a letter from him on 21st of August so I wrote him on the 24th. I got it returned yesterday marked "killed in action" on the 29th. I am in an awful state about Harry. He told me that he would never come back. Poor Maggie and the bairns! I feel for her in her sad bereavement. He told Jim and I that night before he left that he did not know why he enlisted and left his good wife and bairns. John, he has just gone home a little while before us. This is a cruel war. What a lot of men have been killed about here. It was sad taking out . . . [last page missing].

## Afterword

Now, more than ninety years since World War I ended, none are alive who survived that fearful experience. That war—to end all wars—is a part of history: the weapons, the uniforms, the static horror of battle fought in trenches are obsolete now. Yet the First World War refuses to go away. It has marked all of us who were in any way associated with it, even at two generations removed, through our parents and grandparents.

The books, poems, and artifacts of those four and a half years still speak to men and women who were born long after the war ended. The terrible irony of World War I lives on: that highly motivated idealism led boys and men to volunteer to fight and die in the millions. There lay the obscenity of the square miles of mud, barbed wire, broken trees, and shattered bodies into which were flung battalion after battalion to be slaughtered.

World War I was the culmination of personal war, where men saw the other human beings they killed and saw them visibly dead. Men fought with bayonets, with knives, and even with their bare hands. War had not yet become technology against technology. Death was not the elimination of the enemy through pressing a button but something that one experienced personally—bloody, pathetic, and foul.

Perhaps a new generation more distant from that war will discover the anguish and pain in the lives of those young people ninety years ago and in that discovery will understand the futility of war.

# 11 | A Runaway Lad from Canada

Robert Peat Sinclair, or "Wee Bobbie" as he was affectionately called, was probably a spoiled child. He was the youngest of a family of six, with four older brothers and a sister. The oldest brother, Harry, served at the front in France with the Canadian Expeditionary Forces. John, recently ordained to the Baptist ministry, was the director of a center for newly arrived Canadians in East Winnipeg. George was a hired hand at the local railroad shop. Willie was a semiemployed day laborer, and Martha, a clerk at the Hudson Bay Store.

Mother Sinclair, of moderate stature, on the stout side with a beautiful face, was fifty-eight years of age but in poor health. Father Sinclair, a carpenter robust in health, had just turned sixty. He was short in stature, rather abrupt in manners, and the stern ruler of the household.

The family had settled in a worker section of Winnipeg, surrounded by other immigrant families from Great Britain and eastern Europe. Their home was a modest two-story structure that they were buying on a long-term bank mortgage. They worshipped at Elim Chapel, a nondenominational congregation that had roots in the Congregational tradition.

Wee Bobbie, now sixteen, was a carefree, quick-tempered, and strong-willed lad. There were often tense moments when Father laid down the law to his youngest son. Bobbie would simply be silent, sulk, and walk away. His schoolteacher reported him truant more than once a month. He spent more and more time hanging around the general store and got involved with some rough older fellows. He would come home late when he could have been helping his father finish up some rush job.

One day after a disagreement with his father over his house chores, he simply walked out of the house and didn't come home to sleep that night. The next day, he slipped into the house, put a few clothes in an old suitcase, and left town. The family thought he would come back when he got hungry. But on the third day, Father Sinclair reported his absence to the police. Their records did not show any reports of a ruddy-complexioned, slightly built sixteen-year-old being cited for any misdemeanors. Bobbie had clearly skipped town.

It was only a forty-mile hike along a busy highway to the border with the United States. A person could take a shortcut around the border crossing post and walk undetected into the United States from Canada with little trouble. Bobbie was soon hitchhiking to Chicago. A buddy had given him an address of a relative who would "connect him with the right people"— whatever that meant.

His contact, "Butch" Gardini, was the head of a bunch of young hoodlums that operated a pickpocket gang near plush downtown apartments and small businesses. Bobbie was given a bunk bed in a damp basement room. It was quite a shock after the comfortable bedroom at home that he shared with his brother. One of the first conditions to being a part of the gang was to create a new identity, which meant changing your name by obtaining a false birth certificate and address. Since Bobbie was nearly broke, Butch paid his fee but made him sign a paper indicating that he would pay him back within thirty days. After the gang had voted him in, his thumb was nicked slightly to produce enough blood to prove he was now a brother and would, under the threat of grave punishment, never disclose the gang's password.

His new name, which was selected by the gang leader, was an aristocratic name, "Charles Fairfield Robertson." His new birth date was September 11, 1901, and the place of birth, Perth, Scotland. This data had been stolen from a gang member's relative who lived in a distant city. Bobbie was told that he would use the new name, birth date, and address to later apply for U.S. citizenship and obtain a British passport.

With little experience in the art of the pickpocket racket, he was easily nabbed by the police on his first job. Fortunately, he was let go after spending a night in the county jail. He confessed to the judge that he had committed the act only because he was dead broke and hungry. He was not kept in jail, because it was overflowing that week with inmates. Bobbie seemed the less dangerous kid to let go, and he had no police record. After a stern lecture from the judge, he was back on the street.

After a conversation with a disgruntled buddy who was planning to leave the gang, Bobbie realized that the gang was not a good place for him. He needed to get out of town quickly. His buddy had ridden the rails from Texas to Chicago the month before and told him it was no big deal to ride a freight train across country to San Francisco, where there was plenty of honest work. It was early fall, and the weather wouldn't be bad unless they hit frigid days crossing the snowfields of the Rocky Mountains in Colorado and Wyoming.

The lowest-level job—dishwasher—seemed to be the

only place to start with an honest job in that great metropolitan city. The pay was poor, but the food was good. The owner gave him a bed and a locker to store his meager possessions. For the first time in months, Bobbie felt safe and secure. He started to pick up a few words of Mandarin as he listened to the cook and waiters chatter in broken Spanish and rapid Mandarin.

One of the more enterprising workers in the restaurant was attending a public-funded night school near Chinatown. Bobbie learned quickly that, in the labor market, unless he got a GED certificate his chances for employment were minimal. So after a long day of work, he found a couple of hours two nights a week to attend classes. He was a bright young man and caught on quickly to math, science, and history. He also took a typing class. Often, he would prop a textbook over the dish tub and memorize the math tables and prepare for the next history quiz.

When he received his GED, he enrolled in a community college to learn basic secretarial skills. He found a newspaper ad for an opening at the local judge's office for a typist clerk. Since he had a good command of English, he was hired without any references. He also told the judge that he was from Canada and was new in town. He become very interested in the cases that the law office handled, especially the cases related to the violations of immigrant laws.

"Charles," as Bobbie was known, was also interested in the new labor laws and the labor organizations that were just getting organized in California. Since he was the son of a carpenter whose rights were not yet protected in Canada, he understood the pressures of laboring people to get protection from unscrupulous contractors. He was a better clerk in the law office because he understood the challenges faced by those who struggled to earn a living.

As he worked in the law office, he knew that he was a resident alien, living under an assumed name and carrying a forged birth certificate. Would he ever be able to come clean? Yet he kept telling himself to remember that he was Charles F. Robertson and forget that he was ever Robert Peat Sinclair. He often awoke, however, thinking about his father, mother, brothers, and sister. Was my father really that bad? Did John and Clara ever have any children? Did my eldest brother survive the Great War?

Bobbie chose to live out his life in this new land as Charles Fairfield Robertson, born in Perth, Scotland, on September 11, 1901. Under that name he was admitted to prelaw studies at the University of California at Berkeley and then upon graduation to the law school. By 1928, he had passed the exams to be a member of the California State Bar. He specialized in immigrant law, knowing all the while that he was one of those "illegals" who had entered the United States secretly. Would his real identity ever be discovered?

Little by little, he carved out a niche in middle-class America. He also began to return to the faith of his childhood. Since he had attended Sunday school regularly at the Elim Chapel in Winnipeg, he knew the Bible stories and the Gospel hymns. Sometimes, as he would walk in the park on a Sunday, he would sit in the back pew of the Herald Street Baptist Church and listen to the service. He felt comforted by the hymns and the prayers and remembered the teachings he had received in Sunday school and the prayers he said at his mother's knee.

While in law school, he had an internship in a law office where he met a lovely woman of Japanese descent. Her name was Akiko Samuro. She was a *nisei,* which meant that she had been born in the United States and so was a U.S. citizen. She was a member of a Baptist congregation in the Bay Area, and they were married in 1930 by her pastor. She was twenty-five, and "Charles" had just turned twenty-nine on September 11. They purchased a lovely suburban home in San Rafael. He had made it.

As the years rolled by, he took on difficult cases related to the defense of U.S. citizens of Japanese ancestry in the early 1940s, civil rights cases during the 1950s, and Vietnam draft resistor litigations in the 1960s. He became known as a civil rights lawyer who was ready to use his legal skills to protect human rights in any kind of case.

At his retirement banquet in 1976, after the toasts and speeches about his illustrious career with the law firm and several references to cases that he had won before the Supreme Court, the speaker of the day was introduced. He was a lawyer from Arizona who had been invited to speak on the subject "A New Challenge to Immigration Law: The Sanctuary Movement of the Churches."

Charles had heard about this emerging movement but never really took it seriously. The facts were now laid out clearly before the audience: several churches and synagogues had given sanctuary to people from El Salvador who claimed that their request for political asylum had not been accepted by the U.S. government. They were to be deported unless some institution offered them sanctuary. Churches, including a few Presbyterian congregations, were actually harboring in their buildings the political refugees. The churches claimed that they were honoring the century-old tradition of the Jewish and Christian religions to offer a place of refuge to persons who were unable to secure justice through the legal system of the nation.

In his retirement he became one of the first pro bono lawyers to offer his services to defend the Salvadoran immigrants who sought sanctuary in the churches of the Bay Area. On a visit to the Baptist church he attended, he heard a minister from El Salvador tell about the terrible situation there regarding the gross violation of human rights. He also learned that the U.S. government was supporting the military government there with millions of dollars of military aid and training missions.

A ruling by a U.S. circuit court had opened the way for basic changes in the immigration policies of the U.S. State Department in relation to the protection of "those whose lives were in danger because of a threat to their personal liberties in their country of origin."

Charles gave the final years of his retirement to the cause of protecting the undocumented aliens who were at the mercy of the courts of his adopted homeland. The annals of jurisprudence of this nation have recorded the significant contributions that he made to the protection of the human rights of undocumented aliens and the right of religious institutions to offer protective sanctuary until the courts could determine the status of the alien.

In his bank security box upon his death was found a sealed envelope marked: "To be opened by my family after my will is probated in court, my assets distributed according to my will, and my ashes scattered on the waters beneath the Golden Gate Bridge."

Dear family:

I want to share with you the true story of my life. I love each of you dearly, and it is with great remorse that I must disclose to you who I really am. I do this in the Presence of God, whom I trust will forgive me for hiding the truth from you. God is my witness that this story is true.

My real name is Robert Peat Sinclair, the youngest son of Henderson Sinclair and Martha Peat Sinclair. I was born June 1, 1901, in Glasgow, Scotland, where you will find my birth recorded and my name appearing in the census records of 1905.[1] I ran away from home after a disagreement with my father in September 1917 and went to Chicago, where I assumed a new name, "Charles Fairfield Robertson." This name was given to me by a gang that I joined briefly there, and I was involved in petty crime. Since it was soon clear to me that there was no future in that kind of life, I went to San Francisco, where I worked in a restaurant and then went to night school and received a GED and on to college and law school.

You know the story of my career with the firm Roberts, Clive and McDougal. During those years, my personal identity was never challenged, nor did I dare reveal my true identity.

I know that I have sinned grievously against God and against each of you. I can only ask God's forgiveness and your pardon. I do not deserve your forgiveness but trust only in God's mercy and your love.

I have been burdened all my professional life with the knowledge that I was an illegal alien who was championing the cause of other illegal aliens. It was the only path I could walk—trying to shrive my soul—by working to help others find their rightful place in this wonderful nation. How else could I live out my life that was built on so many lies?

Please share this letter with my relatives who may still be living in Canada or elsewhere. I have only these words of counsel to the younger generation of my family and friends: *Do not run away from your problems. Face them honestly and with courage. Be truthful in all you say and do.*

May God have mercy on my soul.

I love you all,

Robert Peat Sinclair

# 12 | The Life and Service of a YMCA Urban Staffer

The Robertson Clan is the oldest family in Scotland and the sole remaining branch of the royal house that occupied the throne of Scotland during the eleventh and twelfth centuries. The story of their relationship to the Sinclairs in Scotland has many connections across the centuries. One story unfolds in the twentieth century in the United States and is of a relative, George Struan Robertson, whose life was grafted into the Sinclair story.

George, born in 1898, was the son of Charles Fairfield Robertson, a mill worker in Terre Haute, Indiana, and Marie Calhoun Duncan. His father mysteriously abandoned the family when George was two years of age, leaving his mother with four small sons, Alexander, eight; William, six; Peter, four; and George, two. According to the family, Charles went to Chicago to find a better job and never came back. They had no relatives or friends there and could not trace the family breadwinner, so Marie valiantly went to work in the cotton mills, leaving her children in the care of a younger, unmarried sister. The little family survived through the support of the local Baptist congregation, of which "Ma" Robertson was a faithful member.

As the youngest son, George was the object of his relatives' and older brothers' loving concern. He was endowed with a strong body, a quick mind, and a subtle sense of humor, even as a small boy. The family's financial needs caused him, however, to drop out of school at fifteen and go to work as a carpenter's apprentice. When he was seventeen, he enlisted in the U.S. Army, declaring that he was eighteen years old. The recruiter did not challenge his statement, because of the bonus incentive for signing up another soldier.

George was tall, muscular, and self-confident. His unit was sent over to France in early 1917 and saw action on the western front for several months before the end of the war in November 1918. He rarely spoke with his family about his army service, because the memories were too painful.

Upon his return to Terre Haute, he was fortunate to find employment as a junior staffer at the local Young Men's Christian Association (YMCA). The congregation belonged to the more progressive and socially conscious wing of the Baptist community, who gave strong support to youth programs in the community. George showed leadership potential and became a star track athlete, especially in long-distance running. He was nominated by the YMCA board for a scholarship at George Williams College, the training school for YMCA career staff.

His first position with the Y was with the downtown Chicago YMCA, which operated a summer camp program on Lake Taneycomo near Branson, Missouri. By 1934, he had moved up to be the athletic director of the camp. It had no swimming pool, so the camp used the beach on Lake Taneycomo, which they shared with Presbyterian Hill on the south side of the lake. This group of cottages and assembly hall housed the continuing education program for pastors of the Presbyterian seminary in Omaha, Nebraska.

The Sinclair family of five daughters, ages twelve through

twenty, and a ten-year-old boy spent their summer vacations at Presbyterian Hill, where their pastor father earned credits toward an advanced theological degree.

George met his future wife, Catherine Sinclair, on the lakefront as they both were supervising young swimmers. She was twenty, and he was thirty-seven. Catherine had already enrolled in the St. John's School of Nursing at the University of St. Louis. She, as the eldest in the family, was mature for her age. The romance blossomed that summer, and George (the owner of a stylish coupe) asked permission to visit Catherine at the family home in Kansas when his summer duties at the Y were finished.

An agreement was soon reached with Catherine's parents. They would approve of her engagement to George only if she finished two years of nursing education before they were married. The years flew by, and the two lovers found ways to keep in touch since Chicago and St. Louis were not that far apart. They were married by Catherine's father on a sweltering Sunday in the summer of 1936.

Because of his maturity and strong record as a summer camp director and winter urban athletic coach, George moved up in the YMCA organization and became executive director of the East Chicago Y, which had ten full-time staffers and over fifty volunteers. He became involved in the local Rotary Club and was a founding member of the first March of Dimes in the late 1930s in the fight against polio. He was also an active member of the reform wing of the Democratic Party, which began to unravel the web of political corruption in the larger Chicago area. As the summer programs grew, there was need for a summer camp nearer to the Chicago area. This led to the purchase of Camp Mohican on the shores of Lake Okalona in eastern Indiana, only sixty miles from the Chicago area.

Life moved forward for Catherine and George as they purchased their first home and became the parents of two sons, Ian and Roderick. The mystery surrounding the disappearance of George's father was rarely if ever mentioned but always present in their minds and hearts. The family felt sure that some day they would discover what happened to him. Ian and Roderick remembered only the family story that their grandfather went to Chicago and never came back.

The Sinclair family gathered in 1997 in Vancouver, British Columbia, for its biannual meeting. One of the relatives brought along a copy of an old letter that he had received from a distant cousin. It was from someone who claimed that he was Robert Peat Sinclair, the youngest son of Henderson and Martha Peat Sinclair of Winnipeg. In the letter, the writer, now deceased, claimed that he had lived under the alias Charles Fairfield Robertson since he left home for Chicago in 1917. The letter had been found in his safe box in the 1980s with the note "To be opened upon my demise."

Ian Charles Robertson, now fifty-three years of age, immediately shouted out: "That was the name of my grandfather, who abandoned my father's family in 1898, when my father was two years old. We never heard from him, and some local people always just said, 'He went to Chicago.' Could he have been killed and someone have falsely obtained his death records and assumed his name as an alias?"

The mystery of his grandfather's death was now revealed. His identity had been stolen and assumed by Robert Peat Sinclair.

Ian, nearly out of breath, continued: "Then my mother, Catherine Sinclair, was the niece of Robert Peat Sinclair, and my father, George Struan Robertson, was the son of Charles Fairfield Robertson, who disappeared in Chicago in 1898. The Sinclairs and the Robertsons are really related!"

# 13 | A Scot in China

Alexander Sinclair and his family were little different from dozens of their neighbors. They were poor dirt farmers recently having received the title to a small plot of land and croft house. They shared tools and labor with the Caleb Hendersons, who lived on the next croft. By hard labor, thrift beyond imagination, and the providential care of their Creator, life was tolerable, if not even pleasant at times.

The heart of the little rural community was the parish church and school and their pastor and teacher, James Sutherland. Every Sabbath, the congregation faithfully intoned the Psalms of David, which their ancestors had sung in that sacred place for centuries. The neighbors greeted each other with the Sabbath kiss after they had arrived at the churchyard and tethered their horses and carts. In the homily each Lord's Day, the minister announced the Promises of God and the Assurance of Salvation. He reminded them that God's way was the only way and to not even think of straying from the holy path.

Into this peaceful world came sadness more often than not. The Sinclair family was struck dumb by the sudden death of their wife and mother when Alexander was only eight years old. It was a dreaded epidemic, referred to locally as "the plague," that silently, but fatally, had crept into the mud walls of the croft house or wafted through the lovely hills and vales.

---

Cf. John Hersey, *The Call* (New York: Alfred A. Knopf, 1985).

Modern medicine, although more advanced in the cities, had not reached the scattered villages of the Highlands in 1908.

Alex's mother was only thirty-four when she was taken from the closely knit family. The burial was in the semifrozen ground of the church cemetery in December. Father William gathered his brood of four—Alex, 8; Jane, 7; Peter, 5; and Lisa, 3—and bravely faced the future through heartbreak and tears. Yet in their sadness, the family was surrounded by the love, compassion, and practical help of their neighbors. They drew strength from a deep faith in a loving God. Their father repeated to his children the Sinclair clan motto: "Commit thy work to God."

It was cousin Maggie Mattison who was the first to offer help to William Sinclair as he looked to an uncertain future for his children, especially the eldest, Alex.

"My dear cousin, let me take in your son Alex to our home in Wick," Maggie offered. "He can attend school nearby and help us in the late afternoon and evenings with our little eating business we have in our home. You can help us with his food by sending in some produce as you may be able. My husband has a steady job at the loading dock at the harbor, so we'll make it alright even with another mouth to feed."

"Maggie, how can I thank thee enough for this kind offer? I have always been pleased with the good manners of Alex. He's a good wee laddie," said William.

"Since Sandy and I have never had children, we'll just treat him like a son," Maggie replied. "You know that we attend the Baptist congregation, so he'll be kept in the ways of the Lord."

Since Alex was too young to be called up for military service in World War I, he was permitted to begin his studies after secondary school at the Glasgow Bible College. He worked in the kitchen to pay for his room and board. The Lady Paton Scholarship Fund provided his tuition of fifty pounds a year. He found a spiritual home in the Kelvinside Baptist Mission in Maryhill. There, he joined the Christian Endeavor Society, accompanied the young people in their street meetings on Saturday evenings, and was supported by a circle of older and younger friends. He also discovered that he had distant cousins, the Fairlies, in Glasgow who were about his age.

Faith in a loving God during those weary war years, even though filled with sadness and stress, gave him a sense of purpose in life. He did not know where God would lead him, but he was building a firm faith, receiving a good education, and being encouraged by his church friends.

He was only nineteen as he approached graduation in 1920. Leticia, two years younger, was the daughter of an old aristocratic Glasgow family. The couple enjoyed long walks together in the gloaming through the Botanical Gardens and along the banks of the Kelvin River. Pastor Anderton kept a watchful eye on this budding romance as he led the youth in their spiritual and social activities.

Alex did not feel called to be a pastor, yet he wanted to serve God in some way. Pastor Anderton suggested that he consider the teaching profession as a way to serve God, perhaps on the mission field. A speaker came to the Glasgow YMCA and spoke about openings for staff in China. There, the YMCA was beginning new social programs that included a literacy campaign. The British and Foreign Bible Society had joined with the YWCA in recruiting teachers to go to China to work in that program. Was this God's call? Would Leticia hear the same call?

There were long conversations with Pastor Anderton and Leticia's parents about their engagement, marriage, and service as teachers in China. They were so young yet so eager to find a place to serve the Lord. It seemed best for them to spend two years at the Teacher's College at the University of Glasgow taking the basic course in teaching methods. After that, her parents were willing to give their permission for her to marry Alex. At the ages of twenty and eighteen, the two young Scots made a pact with God, their parents, and the Bible Society that they would attend Teacher's College for two years, get married, and then to go to China.

The two years at Teachers' College went by rapidly as the young idealists studied and shared dreams of an exciting adventure together in a far-off land. They knew that antiforeigner attitudes prevailed in China. In 1908 during the Boxer Rebellion, 129 missionaries had met their deaths. Even though Christianity in the modern era had been introduced by Rev. Robert Morrison in 1807, who had translated the Bible into Mandarin, there was still much resistance to the foreigners' religion.

The marriage ceremony at the mission chapel was lovely in its simplicity. Their trunks were soon packed with gifts and equipment provided by the Glasgow YMCA and church friends. There was a teary farewell as the newly married couple boarded the SS *Doric* for the six-week voyage to Shanghai, which took them through the Suez Canal and across the Indian Ocean and the China Sea. They docked on the Bund in Shanghai on November 15, 1922, where they were warmly received by a senior member of the YMCA staff. They spent a few days there with the association and were presented with a folding bed as a wedding gift.

They were fortunate to spend the hot months studying the language at the missionaries' summer retreat in Kuling, in the mountains upriver on the Yangtze. The report on Alex's language program is recorded in a memo to the general secretary of the Shanghai YMCA:

Dear Brother,

I have examined Mr. Sinclair in his study of the Chinese language. He has made amazing progress. He has prepared sixty lessons in Mateer, twenty in Kuan Hua Chih Nan, the Gospel of Mark, ten selected hymns, wrote three hundred characters, could carry on free conversation, recite the Ten Commandments, and has memorized ten Chinese proverbs.

Very cordially yours,

E.Y. MacLeish

Leticia was struggling with a Chinese-language tutor at home to learn just enough to oversee the household, shop in the market with a servant, and deal with her first pregnancy. In November 1923, an eight-pound son arrived to gladden their household. The first thing the *amah* did was bathe the baby in water in which she had boiled an acacia bough to give the infant vigor and make it disease resistant. David was relieved simply to find that baby William Cameron had ten fingers and ten toes.

As Leticia adjusted to Chinese customs, she became very concerned about the foot binding of little girls. Once, she asked a Chinese friend, Mr. Lin, to take her to see a professional foot binder work on a young girl's feet. He said it would take some arranging but could be done. A couple of weeks later, he took Leticia and Alex to a modest house in the city. A binder had come for her monthly visit to wash and rebind the feet of an eight-year-old girl who was sitting on a *k'ang,* or brick bed. Leticia asked how long the binder had been working on the girl's feet. Two years, Mr. Lin replied. The binder unwound the wide bandages, and the "golden lilies" were uncovered. Leticia turned deathly pale at the sight but remained silent. The toes had been relentlessly curled back under the soles. Then the foot binder rewound the same bandages tighter than before because each month's binding must turn the "little petals" farther back.

When the girl was fully grown, according to Mr. Lin, her feet would be very beautiful—measuring a span of not more than four inches. And then he added, "She will walk like a willow, for no man with money will marry a girl with flapping feet."

Not long after that, she joined the Anti-Footbinding Association, led by one of her English students. He had gone to the elders of his family and asked that any girls he might have be spared from this custom. He admitted that he had gotten the idea from the missionaries.

He said to Leticia, "I can learn from you. I hope you can

learn from me. And you know that I am the one whose country is at stake."

Leticia became deeply committed to fighting with him against this criminal practice. In time, she came to know much more about the practice and was almost sorry that she did. It was nearly too much to bear, especially as she cradled her first child.

Alex increased his efforts to educate the community. At the Tientsin municipal council, he gave a lecture to the educators of the city on the subject of electricity. He mounted an ambitious lecture that demonstrated the sending of telegraph messages across the campus. It was a great success, and he was invited to give a second lecture on the use of chemical fertilizer on winter wheat. Soon, he was welcomed into the educational community and had an opening to introduce the pilot literacy program.

This program was designed to meet the needs of illiterate laborers who had fixed hours of manual labor, lived under military discipline, and therefore had no pressing need to provide for their families. Oxford-trained educator Johnny Wu had worked with a similar program during World War I in France. There, thousands of Chinese day laborers were brought in to serve under the British army, thus releasing soldiers to go to the front.

The curriculum included teaching the men one thousand characters, which were enough for writing a simple letter and reading the headlines in the newspapers. Their textbook was a scientific reduction of a basic vocabulary, known as *The Peoples One Thousand Characters Lessons,* divided into twenty-four lessons. Each lesson had three parts: a drawing, a simple text using the words, and a checklist of common errors in using the words. The British and Foreign Bible Society was very supportive of this program because of widespread illiteracy. The task before the small cadre of teachers was formidable. Alex was challenged to recruit, train, and support the Chinese district coordinators for the program.

Over the next ten years, the program flourished, even amid some hectic months when an anti-Christian association organized meetings and demonstrations in China's larger cities. By 1924, the nationalist movement had turned against the missionaries and the Christian church. Missionaries were accused of abusing Chinese sovereignty and cultural sensibilities. At the height of the anti-Christian campaign of 1927 to 1928, when Protestant missionaries were leaving the interior of Shandong Province, the Sinclair family stayed on in the village of Peitaiho.

Alex's friend Mr. Wang, who invented labor-saving devices for farmers, had invented a large wooden machine that vastly simplified drawing up water from wells for irrigation. He let out the machines on a system of rentals in kind—for grain or for money. Wang had once been a laborer and got his start through the literacy program. He said that his attitude changed markedly one day when a farmer came to him after a literacy lesson and said: "I can read and write all the characters in your books, but my stomach still growls just like my neighbor who cannot read at all."

Alex began to discuss with Mr. Wang, his fellow teachers, and Johnny Wu a broader program than the basic literacy campaign. With the help of Johnny, they mapped out a three-fold expanded program that included publishing practical materials about rural improvement, dissemination of modern scientific agricultural methods adapted to local Chinese conditions, and modern citizenship training to raise the moral level of the farmers. He and his colleagues had to face the question, Should Christianity be used also as an instrument for social reform?

This new program was seen by some of the leadership of the literacy campaign as a departure from its main purpose. These more conservative leaders felt such an expanded program was a departure from the missionary intent of the program. It was viewed with suspicion as being humanistic and not missionary. Alex was caught between his own personal call to be a missionary and the imperative demands of the Christian to respond to the poverty, corruption, and greed he experienced all around him.

The YMCA had become a Chinese national institution, and the new China looked up to it and believed it was an instrument for the training of Chinese manhood. The Chinese Communist Party was becoming increasingly powerful, however, and spoke out against all foreign cultural invaders. The future of the Sinclair family seemed not to be affected, though, since they were in a remote village and were accepted by their Chinese neighbors as welcomed guests.

The marriage of Alex and Leticia was now blessed with four healthy young boys, ages eight through fourteen. The older two were soon thought to be ready for high school. Should they be sent away to Shanghai to the school for foreign national children? The parents felt that there they would be away from Christian influences and caught up in the temptations of an urban setting. The other alternative was to send them back to Scotland to a school just for missionary children. There, they would also be closer to their relatives and would be able to adjust more easily to life away from their parents. It was going to be a hard decision.

Leticia was also beginning to fray from the pressures of isolation in the village, away from her expatriate friends, and the burden of running the household when her husband was away for long periods. She was now thirty-five years old and had been married to Alex for nearly fifteen years. In addition, she was home-schooling the boys. She began to show signs of unhappiness, which took its toll on her relationship with her husband.

On a bleak winter day after Alex had returned from a long tour of the village literacy schools, their seventeen-year-old Chinese maid, Ma Lee, came to Leticia with a problem: the lock on her door was broken, and she felt insecure staying there alone. Leticia asked Alex to go down and take a look at the lock to see if it was something simple that he could fix. He picked up his toolbox and knocked on Ma Lee's door.

She peered out the window to see who was there and called, "Just a minute until I get dressed."

Either Alex did not hear what she said or did not think that it mattered, so he opened the door and walked in. She was alarmed to see him enter.

"Sir," she said, "please step outside for a couple of minutes, and I'll be ready."

What happened next changed the Sinclairs' fate in China. According to Alex, he reached out to shake her hand and instead touched the loose belt of her bathrobe inadvertently, thus exposing her naked body. She was stunned, and Alex clumsily exited the room, saying that he would come back later and fix the lock.

Later that morning, Ma Lee did not appear in the kitchen at the appointed time. Leticia went to check on her and found a hastily penned note on her bed: "I have had to return home quickly because I learned that my mother is ill."

Of course that was not the reason. Ma Lee told her parents that the master had come into her room and humiliated her. The story moved quickly to the neighbors and filtered back in several versions to the missionary household. Her irate father appeared at the missionary residence within hours and demanded an apology, saying that his daughter's honor had been violated and that she would no longer be permitted to work in his household. One neighbor simply dismissed the story with the ancient proverb: "Here is wood, and there is a spark. Why be surprised when a flame is kindled?"

There were letters sent back and forth to the field office and a cable exchange with the office in Edinburgh. It was clear that the Sinclair family could not remain in China and should be brought home on an early furlough.

The rest of the story unfolded in a small Highland village where Alexander continued his teaching vocation as schoolmaster. The stated reason for their early return from China was that the family needed to bring their older sons back to Scotland for their high school education. Only many years later did the real story behind their recall come to the surface through Chinese acquaintances.

In the early 1980s, William Cameron Sinclair, the eldest son of Alexander and Leticia, was firmly established in the political structure of Great Britain. He had been seated at the age of forty as a member of parliament from one of the Highland districts. He had risen in stature as a member of the committee on foreign affairs and had earned a degree from Oxford University in political science. Since he had been born in China and had kept up the language through high school and college, he was in line for a diplomatic post in China.

In 1982, at the age of fifty-nine, Mr. Sinclair was appointed ambassador to the People's Republic of China. Naturally, he was interested in visiting places where he had lived as a boy before the family returned to Scotland. He stopped in Peitaiho to visit the old house where he had grown up and met a Chinese woman in her sixties who remembered the Sinclair family.

She commented briefly: "Oh, yes, I remember your mother and especially your father. The family was beloved by us all, but they left so suddenly that we didn't have the chance to bid them a proper farewell. We were so sorry to see them go."

# 14 | A Young Pastor and His Bride Respond to God's Call

## Early Friendship, Courting, and Marriage of John and Clara

In the late 1880s, Maryhill was a new housing development in West Glasgow laying along the Great Western Road. This working- and middle-class neighborhood attracted village and rural families that migrated from both the Highlands and the Lowlands seeking employment and a better life for their children.

Clara Mill's family were originally weavers from Perthshire who had settled in nearby Motherwell. Clara was the youngest child and had two older brothers. Her father was a bookkeeper at a chandler supply business on Clyde Bank. John Sinclair's parents came to Glasgow from the Caithness fishing village of Wick in the far north of Scotland. They had seven children, among them were two older boys, Harry and John, who were eleven and thirteen.

This period of Scottish history saw a sharp decline in the rural economy and a dramatic increase in industrialization. Glasgow had become the vital manufacturing hub of the nation, and its population had grown from 200,000 in 1860 to over 1 million in 1900.

The Mill and the Sinclair families lived six blocks apart in Maryhill on Stratford and Dunard streets. The children attended primary school until they earned a labor permit at the end of

---

Cf. John Henderson Sinclair, *In All Faith and Tenderness* (Roseville, MN: privately printed, 2003).

their sixth year. Then it was off to work to help support the family. John got his first job as a telegraph messenger at the Glasgow Exhibition in 1900 at the age of thirteen. Clara went to work at twelve as a helper in an office that hired domestic servants for wealthy families.

Even though industrial smoke and congestion was everywhere in Glasgow, there was also an atmosphere of culture. The botanical gardens along the Kelvin River and the graceful bell towers of Glasgow University lent an aristocratic cast to what might have been a dreary urban landscape. On Sunday, when the industrial furnaces were shut down, the distant Lomand Hills north and east of the city could be seen. Glasgow lived up to its name "auld reeky" because of the smoke pollution, but the city was not without a unique charm.

The Baptists reached out to the new families that came into this great city from the villages and crofts. They established several city missions, one being the Kelvinside Baptist Mission on St. Margaret's Road, which the Sinclair and Mill children attended. Pastor Andrew Bean and his lovely wife, Catherine, had just begun their ministry and quickly attracted a following of children and youth.

Scotland was awash in evangelical piety in the 1890s as the revival campaigns of American evangelists Moody and Finney swept through the churches of Great Britain. There was no television, radio, or movies to fill the few leisure hours of working children like John and Clara. They did little else but work seventy hours a week and attend the services of the mission in the remaining hours.

There were occasional outings in the countryside for the

young people and always some moments for John and Clara to take a brisk walk along the Kelvin River. Their walks usually took place in the gloaming hours, which in the summer lasted until eleven and twelve in the evening.

The early years of the 1900s were times of both joy and sorrow for these teenage sweethearts. Clara's older brother, Alex, became John's pal, which made her friendship with John even more interesting. The three would often stroll together after the Sunday evening Christian Endeavor Society meeting. Alex had the good fortune of being taken on as an apprentice in an architectural firm when he was fifteen, which offered him a promising career.

John's home was saddened by the death from consumption of his beloved sibling Jamesina at the age of twenty-three. Clara's mother died suddenly of heart failure at the early age of fifty. Clara had to take charge of the housekeeping for her father and older brothers when she was only seventeen. Father Mill was fortunate to have a steady income at a shipping company on Clyde Bank.

Hard times came when Father Sinclair and elder brother Harry, both carpenters, were without work for months. John brought home a small check as a clerk in a plumbing business where he controlled the inventory and did the accounting. In the evenings he took courses at the local YMCA night school for working adults. He relished the classes and did well in his studies. He wanted to do more with his life than just count nuts and bolts.

John and Alex both loved the study of the Holy Scriptures and the preparation of devotional talks that they were called upon to give periodically at the mission. Each secretly felt that God would call them to prepare for the Christian ministry. They even dreamed of serving as missionaries some day, perhaps in China, Africa, or some other exotic place.

Baptists were pioneers in the world missionary movement. William Carey, a lay Baptist preacher, had gone out to India in 1793. On the 110th anniversary of that event, the Baptist Federation of Great Britain promoted a recruiting campaign for a new cadre of one thousand missionaries to go out across the world. A missionary who was home on furlough from the Congo Bololo mission visited Kelvinside and presented a stereopticon lecture that deeply moved the youth.

Alex spoke with his father about the ways he could use his architectural skills as a missionary and build churches for the natives in the Belgian Congo. John was more cautious in offering his skills. He was rather shy and not too good with his hands but loved to teach and preach. Maybe he could be used as an evangelist and go to China.

Both young men, now twenty and twenty-one, spoke with Pastor Bean about their interest in preparing for missionary service. Where could they go to study? Could they find scholarships since their families were not able to cover the cost of the studies? Pastor Bean encouraged them and told them to keep praying about their decision to serve God. Often he would say to them, "If it is God's will, God will open up the way."

Within a few months both young men had received application papers from Spurgeon's College (for Alex) and Harley College (for John). Both institutions were in London, and they would be able to see each other during their college years.

Their applications were submitted; interviews in Glasgow were arranged; and requests were made for scholarship aid to wealthy benefactors.

Naturally, Clara followed their conversations with more than casual interest. She always had wanted to be the wife of a minister, but how could she leave her widowed father (then only forty-four years old) and travel to some far-off country? Yet she was content to leave the future in the hands of her fiancé and to God's providence.

Alex was the first to receive a scholarship, from a wealthy woman of the Patton Thread Company. She was one of the early Scottish converts to the Baptist cause and was interested in foreign missions. She made available a fund to help Scottish youth prepare for missionary service, especially those from families who worked in the cotton industry. Even though Father Mill's work was not related to the cotton mills, Alex's application was approved, and he went off to Spurgeon's College in 1906 at the age of twenty-one.

The opportunity for John came two years later when he was offered a place at Harley College, a somewhat less prestigious theological college in London's East End. His scholarship was assured for only two years instead of four, but he eagerly accepted the chance to begin his studies in 1908. By this time he had proposed to Clara, and her father had agreed to their marriage if they would wait until John was ordained and had a pastorate to support a family. Clara's name was now on the waiting list to begin the two-year course at the Ladies' Missionary Training Home in Burnbank, Glasgow.

The two friends, Alex and John, saw a great deal of each

other in London. They found snatches of time between their studies and fieldwork to enjoy all the free attractions of that great city: the British Museum, Westminster Abbey, Hyde Park, and the Parliament buildings—even a peek at Buckingham Palace on the day of the coronation of King Edward VII.

Harley College, more recently founded and bereft of endowment funds to sustain it during hard financial times, announced in the spring of 1910 that it would not be able to open in the fall. What a disappointment for John! He knew, however, that his older brother George and father had spoken of going out to Canada for a year to work. Harry, the eldest son, had gone to British Colombia some years back and found work as a carpenter. Would John be able to go out with his father and George and continue his studies there? Clara quickly thought that her plans to marry John could be advanced and she might go out to become his Canadian bride when he finished three more years of study there. All this made good sense to John— and of course to Clara.

Encouraging word came from the William Sinclair family, who had gone out to Canada in 1882 to homestead. Although Uncle William had failed at farming and met an early death in 1908, his son, David, had succeeded as a bricklayer and building contractor. David was well established there, as well. He sent word that there was work in the housing boom in Manitoba. Martha, John's nineteen-year-old sister, might find a clerking job at the Hudson Bay Company, a large department store.

Manitoba had a large Baptist theological college, Brandon College, where John could finish the final three years of his studies. By May 1910, the trunks of Father Sinclair and two of his sons, George and John, were packed. They sailed from Liverpool on the SS *Hesperian,* arriving in Montreal on June 20, 1910. Mother Sinclair, Willie, Robert, and Martha stayed behind until the following year, when Father had found a house and gotten work in Winnipeg.

What a thrill it was for John to move ahead in his studies for the associate of theology degree, which was required for ordination in the Canadian Baptist Convention. In his memo book of 1910 to 1911, he recorded the schedule for his classes: ethics, biology, Hebrew history, New Testament literature, Greek, English literature, and sociology. Each weekend he traveled by train to the Longburn station, forty miles to the north of Brandon, to preach in a rural congregation.

Manitoba was part of the Wild West of the Canadian frontier. Few letters have survived from his college years, but a large photo of the classroom building and his graduation diploma always hung on his study wall. By today's standards in higher education, Brandon College was a rather ordinary college, but for John it was like a gateway to heaven. He would be the first in his family to receive a college education.

Letters sped across the Atlantic Ocean (three weeks each way) between John and Clara. He was offered a summer pastorate by the Longburn congregation for the summer of 1913. A deacon offered to keep him (and his bride) in his home. There was also a chance for a permanent pastorate in Winnipeg in the fall. The wedding date was set for July in the home of Pastor Marshall in East Winnipeg.

Clara bid a difficult farewell to her widowed father on the Liverpool wharf and sailed alone to the New World. When she disembarked in Montreal twenty days later, the customs agent was concerned about her economic survival in Canada.

"And, young woman, how much money do you have?" asked the agent.

"Oh, just five dollars and my ticket to Winnipeg. But my fiancé, John Peat Sinclair, will meet me at the station, and we're to be married on July 8," replied Clara.

Years later, she told her children, "It must have been my honest face that convinced the agent I would not be a burden to a welfare agency in the nation."

And so it was. Clara arrived safely at the rail station in Winnipeg, but John missed seeing her at first.

His excuse was, "But Clara, you were wearing a different hat!"

In the rush after the wedding, they missed the daily train, so they quietly checked in at the railway hotel and took the first train out the next morning. For a city girl, the experience of living in an isolated farmhouse in the middle of an endless prairie was both memorable and uncomfortable. She soon adjusted to having a husband and her life as a preacher's wife. She often said that this was the life she had always dreamed of.

## The Community Center Ministry in the Immigrant Community

The MacDonald Memorial Institute, located in Eastwood, a workers section of Winnipeg, was a ministry to "newly arrived Canadians," the term used for immigrants. The institute was named after the first Baptist minister in Western Canada. John was named superintendent of the institute in the fall of 1913.

This neighborhood house, as these institutions were sometimes called, served all people regardless of creed or nationality. Visiting a Christmas program at the institute gave a preview of the nationalities of the children who were involved in its programs: Icelandic, Scandinavian, Russian, Dutch, Hungarian, English, and Scottish. A map of the Eastwood area hung on the office wall, with the ethnic neighborhoods marked in colored pencil and the approximate population of each area: English/Scots (1,500), Germans (1,000), Dutch (1,000), Scandinavians (750), Poles/Ruthenians (750).

A Sunday school of over 150 children met in two sessions. The Sunday evening Gospel service was well attended at the nearby Bethel Baptist Church. On late Monday afternoon there was a lantern talk with cultural information and Bible stories for children. During World War I, Thursday evenings were dedicated to a women's meeting for those whose sons and husbands were at the front. The honor roll of the institute had ninety-two stars emblazoned on the red banner. By mid-1915, thirteen of the blue stars were replaced with gold stars to honor the men who had made the supreme sacrifice.

The institute's building on Bigelow Street was a two-storied frame structure. John and Clara lived on the second floor. Their first child, Catherine Grace, was born in August 1914. John had been ordained for scarcely a year when World War I broke out. All British citizens across the far-flung British Empire knew that they would be involved in some way in the war effort. John might be called up to serve as a military chaplain. The young man who lived next door had volunteered, and the son of the deacon at Bethel Baptist Church had been drafted into the medical reserve corps. Two of the leaders of the institute's Boys Brigade informed the pastor that he should start looking for their replacements.

John took very seriously his pastoral responsibilities to those families whose loved ones were at the front. The Canadian Expeditionary Forces suffered heavy casualties during the first two years of the conflict. John would often follow the telegraph delivery boy who delivered the death notices. On some days, the casualties were announced only in the *Winnipeg Free Press*. Each day, John checked the notices on the bulletin board in the post office to be sure he knew about all the families who might be affected. Found among his papers was a frayed old notebook titled "War and Peace" with page after page of news clippings and death notices of the war casualties.

The death of John's eldest brother, Harry, killed at Vimy Ridge, France, in 1917 further saddened the young pastor's household. Harry, a carpenter, was an infantry soldier, aged thirty-four, who left behind a wife and two children of three and five years of age.

Because of John's deep involvement in the lives of the children and youth of Eastwood, a group of citizens approached him and asked if he'd stand for election to the local school board. John was ready for this volunteer civic post but was then informed that the law required all candidates be property holders. As a minister, he lived on church property and could not qualify as a property holder. By 1918, two more little girls, Mona Jamesina and Martha Muriel, had been added to the Sinclair trio.

John and family headed west again after he was contacted

by the Canadian Baptist Convention home office and called to take charge of a newly organized congregation in Cranbrook, British Colombia. Since John always had the missionary spirit, the call seemed just right. A manse was offered for their growing family, now with three little girls, ages two, four, and four months. Cranbrook was a growing town with a booming fruit industry. John and Clara were ready to move farther west.

The Great War was beginning to draw to a close. The nation was facing the problems of the returning veterans, as well as a wave of Hungarian immigrants moving into the fertile valleys of British Colombia. The family of five settled in larger living quarters and the bustle of a new community. John joined the Masonic Order to make contacts with the men of the community. He also organized a boys club. His memo book was sprinkled with some favorite quotations, such as Abraham Lincoln's "I am not bound to succeed but bound to live up to what light I have."

John found great satisfaction in his ministry on the Canadian frontier. This momentary euphoria quickly disappeared, however, when the tragic influenza epidemic descended on the remote rural village of Cranbrook. Schools and churches were closed for several weeks. John's memo book recorded twenty funerals in the short space of three weeks in late October and early November. He buried the young and the old: "funeral of Tommy Martin, age nine . . . funeral of Elder MacDonald, age 76." On November 4, 5, and 6, a funeral was held each day.

The only good news that fatal month came from the long-awaited telegram from the western front which stated that, on November 11, the hostilities had ended. What a week it had been for a thirty-one-year-old pastor. The flu epidemic continued to take its toll into early December: "Baby Clapson, ten days old died. December 1 and three more funerals on December 11."

The postwar years in the Kootaney Valley of British Colombia were filled with new challenges in ministry with the arrival of many displaced eastern European families. Grandfather Mill, widowed since he was forty-three years old, came from Glasgow to live with Clara and John and help with the little children. The fourth daughter, dark haired and complexioned, arrived in May 1920 and received her mother's first and family name—Clara Mill.

The decision was made in June 1920 to move to California. John learned he could complete the coursework for a bachelor's of theology degree at the Pacific School of Religion in Berkeley, for which he needed only two more years of seminary education. He had been assured by the California Baptist Convention that he could find a part-time pastorate in the area that would offer his family a manse while he commuted by train to Berkeley for classes during the week.

An answer came back that a newly organized congregation in Aromas, California, offered a manse and a small stipend for weekend pastoral work. In the late summer of 1920, the family of six moved into the beautiful California weather of the Pajaro Valley. With Daddy being away five days each week, the two years spent in Aromas were hard years for Clara and the four girls, but the congregation was very supportive, especially during the eldest daughter's bout with typhoid fever.

Clara entered these lines in her diary:

I dare not leave the record of our life in Aromas without paying tribute to the church people there. No better could be found. When our daughter lay at death's door, they cared for our children in their homes for many weeks and even paid the wages of a trained nurse to care for our daughter. Since I was expecting our fifth child, one of the ladies made a complete layette for the baby. . . . Yes, Edith Anna arrived—our fifth daughter! Besides a minister's wife and family knowing the joy of friendship with wonderful people, they also receive so many kindnesses of a practical kind that can never be repaid.

In 1923, the Sinclair family, now seven, boarded the train for Belen in the Rio Grande Valley of New Mexico. Along with their trunks was a barrel of canned fruit donated by the fruit growers in the Aromas congregation. Their new parish in Belen was originally a Spanish-American trading post in the late 1700s that was later developed by German-American business people in the late 1800s. A federated church was organized that brought together the Protestants of several denominations. John was called to be their first resident pastor. The Lutherans had built a small chapel and a rather spacious manse. Here was another missionary challenge for John and Clara as they began a ministry of eight years in New Mexico. The delightful climate is eulogized in the state anthem in the lines "Under a sky of azure, / Where balmy breezes blow, / Kissed by the golden sunshine / Is Nuevo México."

They had been away from the old country for nearly a decade and had found the fulfillment of their missionary call on the U.S. frontier. Would they ever return to the land of their birth? Probably not, they reasoned. John had been received as a member of the Presbyterian Church, U.S.A., which had recently established a pension fund for church workers. He became the father of six children with the arrival of a son, John Henderson, in 1924. Clara and John had nearly fulfilled the required five years of residency in their adopted land.

So in 1925, John presented himself in the courthouse in Los Lunas, New Mexico, before a Spanish-speaking county judge to apply for citizenship. After the necessary security checks, he was advised that he would be sworn in. Little did he know he would be required to "foreswear allegiance to all foreign sovereigns."

He thought to himself, "Can I do that? I have been a British citizen under Queen Victoria, King Edward VII, and King George V."

But there was no turning back now. He mumbled yes, but with a deep sigh. In his desk drawer, he always kept his coveted Victoria medal, which he had received for excellence upon graduating from the sixth grade.

A few years later, Clara applied for her citizenship papers. Her experience was equally emotional, but she knew it was the right thing to do for herself, her husband, and her children. When she came home that day, she shut the bedroom door and sang to herself a verse of "God Save the King."

Their second pastorate in New Mexico was in Artesia, a growing town in the Pecos Valley. Artesia had much better schools than Belen and excellent musical programs in both the church and community. A schoolteacher and his wife, Mr. and Mrs. Harp, even organized the Pecos Valley Orchestra, which included four Sinclairs on string instruments, with Mother Sinclair learning to play the string bass.

John and Clara always dreamed that each of their children would earn a college degree. But with a monthly salary of $150, they had no money for college tuition. In the Southwest, few Presbyterian colleges offered tuition scholarships to qualified children of Presbyterian clergy. However, in the Midwest— Kansas, Nebraska, Oklahoma, and Missouri—several colleges offered reduced tuition for the children of Presbyterian ministers, and some also offered students work-study and summer employment.

In August 1931, John traveled through the Midwest in search of a pastorate. An attractive call came from Caldwell, Kansas, a thriving church and community with a large manse and in proximity to several Presbyterian colleges. The family left fair New Mexico for a new state, with a certainly less pleasant climate but with the possibilities of a college education for the six Sinclair offspring.

## Three Core Values of the Family

The daily life of the family was built around three core values: religious devotion, musical education, and high scholarship standards. John and Clara had gone out to work at age twelve and did not have the advantage of musical educations and extracurricular activities. They longed to see their children benefit from these gifts.

As to religious devotion, each weekday after breakfast the family worshipped around the kitchen table. They read from two books, the Holy Bible and the *Yearbook of Prayer for Missions*. All the family then knelt beside their chairs, and Mother or Father prayed. No giggling or smart talk was tolerated; it was worship. Each child was encouraged to pray on their own during the day, as well, which was aided by the Christian Endeavor Society's Quiet Hour. Of course, they were also required to attend Sunday school and morning and evening services at the church—which was always next door!

Thanks to local music teachers' usually offering private lessons at half price for the minister's children, each child learned to play the piano and an instrument. On a few occasions, a Sinclair family orchestra, made up of the six children, preformed at church services. The sound of music could be heard emanating from the Presbyterian manse early in the morning and late at night.

As to scholarship, each child was expected to meet high expectations. Of course, untarnished deportment was taken for granted (weren't these the minister's children?). Father and Mother were always available to help their children with homework. In the evening the children could usually be found clustered around the dining room table under a big lamp doing homework. Even a C+ or a B- was considered less than satisfactory. The challenge was not just to do your best but to do your very best!

Wherever the family lived, a taste of Scotland was evident in their home. A distinct Scottish accent was heard when John or Clara answered the telephone or the doorbell. Upon entering the living room, one would spy a bright tartan-covered songbook above the piano keyboard. On the kitchen wall hung "The Scotsman Calendar," which came in the mail each year from Glasgow, sent by Uncle Gladstone and Aunt Jean.

Over the next twenty-two years, from 1931 to 1953, the Sinclairs served five pastorates in Kansas. The children grew up and moved away from home. The aging couple enjoyed life in the slow lane during their declining years. John's health began to show signs of serious heart and circulatory problems while in his midfifties. He requested early retirement at age sixty-six and died two years later. Clara, gifted with a strong constitution and boundless energy, lived on until the beginning of her nineties.

Their earthly remains lie beside each other in a lovely wooded cemetery overlooking the Delaware River in eastern Pennsylvania. But the memories of their service to God, church, community, and, above all, their children live on.

## 15 | A Scot American with a Passion for Peace and Social Justice

Margaret Sinclair, the fourth child born in Canada, was known as "Scottie" because she wore a classy wool tartan skirt. Even though her parents spoke British English with a decided accent, she was an all-American girl. Her skirt, with its red-, green-, and black-threaded cloth, never seemed to wear out. She often wore it with a white blouse with a Scottie dog embroidered on the collar.

But it was not only the skirt that made Margaret a favorite among her friends. It was the enthusiasm with which she tackled life. She was up to every challenge: wrestling with her brother Johnny on the lawn that spread between the manse and the red-brick church, leading her Girl Scout troop on a hike down a country lane, or being the first girl to climb to the top branches of the old mulberry tree in the backyard.

She was a tomboy—a larger than life girl—in the small-town neighborhood gang. And she would quickly let you know that she was born in Canada—in the far-off Kootenay Valley of British Colombia—even though she had left there with her parents and three big sisters when she was only six weeks old. Her early years were spent in California and in New Mexico, where she started school. The small town had many Mexican-American families. The Sinclair family employed a Mexican girl, Chonita, to help with the six children. Early in life,

---

Cf. Claire (Hurn) Sinclair, *As Way Opens My Life*

(privately printed, 2000).

Margaret was exposed to the life of another culture and to another language.

As a first grader, she loved to play on the "acting bar," which was a piece of pipe attached to the garage and the adjacent power pole in the alley. The plumber had come one day to put it up. She loved to spend hours and hours playing on it, hanging by her knees and doing flips with one knee over the bar and a foot secured behind the other knee. She attended a rodeo one hot, hot summer day, and the sight of horses doing dangerous tricks—and the poor calves being roped and thrown—remained with her as a vibrant memory. Of course, her games as a girl were not just with dolls and baby clothes; she and the neighborhood kids built a cave in a vacant lot near the manse and a miniature golf course in the backyard.

She loved to remember being invited to a family's cabin in the mountains where they tied a gunny sack on a rope to ride across a deep ravine. Either you would jump off on the other side or swing back to be caught at the place you jumped off. The boys taught her to make a bow and arrow and be a "real Indian."

Margaret became a Brownie Scout at age ten and joined the Girl Scouts when she was twelve. The troop met in the "Scout hut," a small cabin next to the city library. Her father put up an iron hoop on the garage behind their home so she could practice basketball. Her girls' basketball team at school officially played by the girls' rules, but often, without a coach, they would play by the boys' rules.

Margaret always looked for a physical challenge. She played tennis with a borrowed racquet until she bought her own using a five-dollar graduation gift. A public swimming pool was available, but it cost ten cents each time. So more often she went swimming with friends at a nearby river that had a rope swing hung from a huge cottonwood tree. She developed into a strong swimmer.

And Margaret was a preacher's daughter—the heir of the pluses and minuses of the flawless behavior expected of all preachers' kids in a small midwestern town. The expectation to be good all the time could be a burden. Annual family vacations in the 1930s to distant corners of her adopted country gave her glimpses of American history and geography.

Margaret was soon off to a church-related college, full of all the idealism that a young woman of eighteen could muster. War clouds were gathering over western Europe, and visiting lecturers—missionaries, peace activists, and literary figures— came to campus. Letters from a missionary uncle and aunt in the Belgian Congo whetted her interest in joining them some-day as a missionary doctor.

Her days were packed with study, classes, dorm parties, and long hours working in the college dining room to pay for her room and board. Soon the nickname "Scottie" fell by the wayside, and she became known as "Margaret" or "M. Sinclair." Her first college boyfriend was the son of missionaries in Gua-temala, and he told her that he also might become a doctor someday, though he certainly would not go back to the prim-itive country of his childhood. He wanted to establish himself in a prestigious practice in a big city.

In her second year of college, Hitler invaded a defense-less neighboring nation. This and other world events cast long shadows over Margaret's idealistic vision of a world without war. She remembered that her Uncle Harry, a Canadian infantry soldier, had been killed in France during World War I. Yet her passion for world peace continued to grow deeper in her mind and heart. She found a few fellow students and professors who shared her vision of a warless world and who took seriously Jesus' teachings on how we should treat our enemies. She wrote in her autobiography: "The teachings of Jesus were important to me and should be translated into nothing less than peace and justice. My greatest desire was to be a part of that translation."

And then there was Jeremy, the tall, handsome boy from Texas. He was the one! He too was full of idealism and personal charm and also wanted to study medicine. Even though he had been reared in a family with much more of the world's goods, Margaret and Jeremy seemed to hit it off. In the week of their graduation, they were joined in marriage in the college chapel by Margaret's father and Jeremy's minister uncle.

Jeremy hoped for a deferment from military service since he was preenrolled in medical school. However, the pressing demand for young men at the front moved the local draft board to cancel his medical school deferment. What should he do? He felt he could not take up a gun to kill another human being. He saw only two routes: cross the border to Canada or apply for status as a conscientious objector (CO). He chose the latter.

The historic peace churches—Quaker, Mennonite, and Brethren—had negotiated a service program with the Selective Service to form units of conscientious objectors to work in the severely understaffed state mental hospitals. The local draft board reluctantly agreed to his reclassification. These draftees were to be fed and lodged by the institution and paid ten dollars a month.

Jeremy and Margaret, recently married and committed to living out their ideals, were soon off to a distant state to begin a difficult testing period in their young lives. Margaret was able to find a low-paying position at the same hospital where Jeremy was assigned. In their search for an apartment, the attitude of the conservative village was less than friendly to this young CO and his wife. But they found a place and survived on "love and a loaf of bread" for two long years.

As the war wore on, Jeremy felt the need to do something more to show he really cared about both civilians and soldiers who were affected by the armed struggle. His favorite cousin was reported missing in action; the boys had spent many happy days together as children. The loss of his cousin and the feeling of being ineffective in the mental hospital unit led him to request reclassification as a noncombatant soldier. He was assigned to a medical unit for a year in Europe, where he served until the war drew to a close in 1945. Again, he felt he was acting according to the dictates of his conscience.

Margaret and Jeremy wanted to have children, settle down in a community, and live a normal life. Four lovely daughters came into their lives and brought them much joy. Their extended families were supportive of the young couple as they found ways to support themselves in farming and complete the required courses to obtain secondary school teaching certificates. Jeremy became a physical education and science teacher. Margaret enjoyed her classes as a biology and chemistry instructor.

Yet the dream of a continuing marriage began to fade as the years rolled by. Jeremy seemed to lose some of his idealism and drifted away from Margaret. There was apparently not enough glue to hold them together. A separation was followed by a divorce. Two lives began to walk down separate roads after nearly three decades of traveling the same road together.

The daughters, all but the one still in high school, were off to college and professional schools at the time of the divorce. Each handled the situation differently but bravely, and all kept in close touch with their mother. The eldest became a college literature teacher; another, a Montessori early childhood educator; a third studied art; and the youngest began as a museologist and then studied nursing. Margaret found a teaching position in a Quaker school for several years and saved enough money to cover her expenses as a volunteer teacher.

Margaret had to forge a new future in midlife and build new relationships. There were some miserable days as she put her life back together. She earned a second teaching degree in primary education since she had done only high school teaching. Good personal discipline and a newfound faith in the teachings of the Society of Friends gave her openings of service in Israel and Palestine and in Kenya with overseas service units of the Quakers.

She spent several years in the Gaza Strip serving as an instructor of Arab refugee mothers in early childhood education. These were years of personal growth as she worked closely with an Arab teacher-translator under less than favorable conditions. She was supported by the American Friends Service Committee in one of their many social work programs around the world. The next assignment was with the British Quaker Service in Kenya, where she worked with Ugandan refugees who had sought asylum under United Nations protection.

In between her volunteer service, she hiked and biked in Scotland and Switzerland. Everywhere she went, her friendly disposition and openness to people of other cultures filled her life with new friends. Her life was enriched by new friends from Japan, Ethiopia, Poland, and Iraq, as well as Scotland and Switzerland.

After several years of exciting and demanding overseas service, Margaret felt that she needed to be closer to her daughters and their families in the United States. This decision led her to the Rocky Mountain states to find employment and lodging with friends from her college years. But again, the wanderlust set in.

She accepted an invitation from friends to study at a Quaker college in England for a short time and then spent several months in Scotland. With her Canadian birth certificate in hand, primary school attendance records in New Mexico, and the naturalization papers of her British parents (she was a British citizen when she was brought to the States as a baby in arms), there was no question that she qualified for joint American and British citizenship. At one time she actually felt that she wanted to settle permanently in Scotland.

The sojourn in Scotland did not turn out well. Several factors caused Margaret to return to the United States, where she was employed as a field representative for the World Association of the Society of Friends. She was designated a "messenger," traveling throughout the western United States and Alaska and visiting local Friends meetings. She immensely enjoyed this chapter of her life, sharing her experiences in Europe, Africa, and the Middle East.

In the Quaker tradition she knew that women always went out to tell the truth as they saw it. That led her to join the movement in Montana to abolish the death penalty. With another woman, Eve Malo, they traveled more than three thousand miles and visited forty-two Montana towns to talk with people. They lived in a sheep wagon towed by a pickup truck, met with local residents, and gathered signatures for a resolution in the state legislature to abolish the death penalty. Margaret was then seventy-nine, and Eve was seventy-one.

In her seventies she paused long enough in her life's journey to write an autobiography. The title of her book, *As Ways Open,* is a phrase often used in Quaker circles to describe the way by which God opens doors during life's journey and beckons us to write new chapters in our life. In these five hundred pages, Margaret has given a fascinating record of six decades of the Quaker experience. The following vignette lifts up the seriousness with which Margaret lived out her life of service:

> Working with the Palestinians in the Gaza strip made me aware that I should always look for "that of God" in the Israel officers and soldiers who were part of my daily life in the refugee camp. On one occasion, the Military Governor of Gaza requested a visit from an officer to one of our day care centers. I could not deny the request. I did ask the officer if he would be willing to remove his side-arms before coming into the

school room. This he did. After an inspection of the facilities, including the picture books the PLO had given us, he sat on the floor and played with the children. He had a five year old of his own! My heart was stretched and I knew the oneness of that Great Ocean in a new way.[1]

Margaret's life of service to human society, her role as a caring and guiding parent, and her enthusiasm for all that is good and true is another proof that the heather as it is scattered drops its seeds, grows, fades away, and yet greatly enriches the soil (see photo section following p. 82).

# 16 | A Seamstress Becomes an Officer in the Women's Auxiliary Army Force

*Barbara Mill's story transpired in far-off Africa and war-torn England during the first half of the twentieth century. Her life is documented in family letters and stories passed down by her parents, relatives, and friends. Some blank spaces in her life story could be filled only by researching missionary archives and rereading the social and political history of the years before, during, and after World War II. The tapestry of her life seems to follow a four-strand design: childhood and adolescent experiences, conflictive adult models, the strains of military service, and a disappointing romance.*

## The Daughter of Missionaries

Barbara's parents, Alexander and Ethel Mill, were pioneer missionaries in the Belgian Congo under the Baptist Missionary Society of Great Britain. They had married later in life than most couples—Alex was thirty-two and Ethel was thirty-seven. Barbara Mary was born on July 31, 1920, in a Roman Catholic hospital in Stanleyville, the colonial capital. Ethel wrote to her family that she was in labor for sixteen hours. Since she did not have enough breast milk for her baby, a goat was brought in from the countryside to provide nourishment.

Barbara was born with a large birthmark on her lower check and upper neck. Though she grew to be an attractive person of moderate stature, with grey eyes and comely features,

---

Cf. John Henderson Sinclair, "The Life of Bandombele and Mama Bandombele of the Congo" (unpublished ms, 1991).

this physical blemish may have had an impact on her demeanor and personality.

Her mother, Ethel Mary Starte, came from a comfortable middle-class merchant family in Cambridge. She was one of the first graduates from the prestigious nurses' training school at Guy's Hospital, London. After an overseas experience in India, she returned to England and accepted the second offer of marriage by her Scottish sweetheart, Alexander Mill—a proposal she had turned down five years before.

Alexander George Mill, a Glaswegian and recently ordained Baptist minister, was tall, handsome, and articulate. They made quite a pair as to stature and personality. He was gregarious, and she was quite reserved. He was poetic and romantic; Ethel was practical and all business. Yet they found a common missionary calling in answer to their spiritual yearnings to serve God and to respond to human needs.

But now with a tiny baby girl in their arms, how could they bring up their daughter in a primitive village in the Congo? They were keenly aware of the problems that faced all children born to missionary parents. This matter was not merely academic, since three male missionaries had recently died and their widows had to return to England. An epidemic of infantile paralysis had swept the district, and twenty-nine native children had died.

The decision was painful, but they both felt that their baby daughter should not remain with them at their mission post. When Barbara was nine months old, Alex accompanied her wife and daughter on the twelve-hundred-mile riverboat trip to the coast, where he saw them off for England—a separation that lasted three years. Their family was reunited in May 1923. The three Mills traveled that year to far-off New Mexico to visit Alex's sister and brother-in-law and their five children.

"What a reunion that was," wrote Alex's sister Clara. "We had not seen each other for over ten years!" Alex also had five nieces whom he had never seen. Different accents filled the New Mexican home: the broad English accent of three-year-old Barbara asking for a "bah-nah-na" as if she were back in Africa and the strange Western twang of her American cousins.

The two couples held closed-door conversations regarding Barbara's future. Could Barbara become a part of her American family, rather than being reared by her relatives in England? It became clear, however, that the logical choice was England since a good boarding school for missionary children, which she could go to when she was six years old, was near her English relatives.

Elsie, Ethel's unmarried sister, seemed the right family member to care for Barbara for the three years until she could be admitted to the school, Seven Oaks. Other Starte relatives were in the Cambridge area, as well, so this decision seemed right. Barbara's separation from her parents after they returned to Africa was surely far more traumatic than the following letter from Elsie revealed:

> Barbara is very happy at Ashwell. Several times I saw her holding her cousin Harvey's hand and walking him around. He is only fourteen months and Barbara looks after him like an older sister. . . . I don't think she realized that you had gone away for a long time

and that Africa is very far from England. It is well as it should be. . . . It is the best for all concerned that she be here with us.[1]

The Mills' next furlough was not until four years later in 1928. Yet Barbara seemed to take to her parents quickly when she saw them again after the long absence. Alex wrote:

As far as Barbara's welcome to us is concerned, there is nothing wanting. She took us as her property as soon as she saw us. After a little quiet shyness she burst into an afternoon of horseplay which only stopped for sleep and renewed early next morning. We are to take her right way to Cambridge for a holiday.[2]

The next year, the family took a vacation to Grenoble, France, for four months. Since Ethel had never had formal instruction in French (Alex was fluent in the language), she had an opportunity to gain more than a nodding acquaintance with the language. Of course, little Barbara picked up the language quickly from her playmates, but for Ethel the French language was always a challenge.

Alex wrote:

We went to the Waterloo battlefield near Brussels and then we saw the great Diarama housed in a domed building beside the great Lion monument. Barbara saw how terrible a battle was and is now strongly in favor of peace. We also saw the great Palais de Justice (the largest in Europe) where 2,000 German soldiers were billeted during the occupation. . . . They scavangered from the buildings all the bronze there for the manufacture of ammunition casings.[3]


Her parents sailed back to Africa in mid-July of 1929. Barbara, then aged nine, returned to Seven Oaks. But she struggled academically. She was interested in flowers, animals, drawing, and sewing more than she was in her basic studies. Ethel wrote to her sister-in-law: "Barbara is no good at studies, but good at art. . . . She shows no reasoning powers."[4] When her parents returned on furlough in 1933 and 1938, they saw Barbara quite often. By age seventeen she had finished her studies at Seven Oaks and enrolled in Barrett's Trade School in London.

Her first job was as a seamstress with a dance company with whom she traveled around Great Britain. Her mother was never pleased with this work since she said that "dancing was the work of the devil." Mother Ethel was a dyed-in-the-wool puritan. Barbara never subscribed to her parents' more conservative religious beliefs. She was a free spirit in many of her ways.

In early 1940, as World War II was beginning, she volunteered for military service in the Women's Auxiliary Army Force. She was assigned as a plotter in the Aeroplane Drawing Office because of her graphic skills. She spent her days developing maps, based on previous air raids, to assist the air defense command in charting possible routes for future air attacks.

This work proved to be too strenuous for her. In March 1940, she was relieved of her office job and assigned to a lonely aircraft watch post in Devon. There, she billeted with a local family, made some friends, and seemed to get along well. Later, she was posted in the Orkney Islands in the far north of Great Britain.

The years of 1940 and 1941 were years of terrible suffering for the people of England. When Barbara was transferred to another aircraft spotter post in Sussex, the blitz hit central London, the financial center of Britain, leaving a square mile of devastation. More than 532 fires on December 27 and 28 gutted London. On May 10, 1941, a 400-plane bomber raid on a bright moonlit night destroyed over 11,000 homes, killed 1,486 people, and wounded another 1,800.

## The Brief Romance with Toby Carter

Toby was a member of a Royal Air Force bomber crew whom Barbara met through friends in the Sussex area. Was Toby on leave for R & R, or was his unit stationed there? Many small airfields were scattered around the countryside. The only record in the family archives is his personal card and inscription: "J. Christopher Carter, Corpus Christi College, Cambridge. With all my love, Toby." (A request by the family after the war sent to the Ministry of Defense ascertained that an RAF veteran by that name was still living and that if the inquirer would identify their relationship, his current address would be provided. The family chose not to contact him.)

Since Barbara had lived in Cambridge for several years in the 1930s, she may have met him while on leave in Sussex, or they may have met through some church activity since his last gift to her was a copy of the new revision of the Bible.[5] It is not clear whether their relationship was a romance or a continuing friendship that Barbara felt was something more.

In a letter from Barbara to her Aunt Clara in America, the story unfolds as far as the family will ever know. The letter carried the inside address "RAF Station, West Prawle, near Kingsbridge, Devon, England":

Dear Aunt Clara,

Toby was reported missing from Singapore, but he is safe and as John, his brother says, "He has been serving in France, Norway, the London blitz and now in Singapore." I think that Toby cannot have completed the purpose for which he was sent into the world just yet, that he should come through all that . . . whatever purpose that may be. Toby does not deserve a death like that—it is only a heroic death because it is so freely accepted by those who meet it as a cause worth fighting for. He does not deserve to be killed by fellow creatures whose minds love beauty. That is why war is so terrible and that is why I must fight it . . . to help those who are the courage to fight for us even against their own hearts . . . and each does it in his own way—pacifist, soldier, sailor, airman and so many other minds with methods all their own. . . .

We have just moved into our new rooms. We are terribly busy and I love it. My rank is equivalent to lieutenant in the army and sub-lieutenant in the navy and flying officer in the air force. I like it but I can only hope that other people like the work I am doing

in the same way. All one can do is try. . . . I have beautiful pinks in my bedroom with a lovely scent. . . .

With all my love to you,

Barbara[6]


Toby survived the war, and according to a family story,
Barbara read in the society pages an account of Toby's marriage. Alex felt that this final blow led to Barbara's nervous
breakdown. Ethel wrote to Clara a rather terse comment: "Toby
wrote that he was married and to forget about him."[7]

Perhaps, the following, fuller story can be imagined.

Barbara was assigned to one of the most remote aircraft
observer posts in Great Britain, on the Island of Papa Westray in
the Orkneys. It could be reached only by the WAAF's commu-
nications motorboat from Kirkwall—two hours away. The only
link with the outside world was a battery-operated shortwave
radio. Her companion was Lt. Fiona Henderson, a twenty-one-
year-old fresh recruit.

On New Year's Day, memories of the past, the loneliness
of the present, and fears of the future seemed to rush in on
Barbara as she tried to pen a letter to her parents in the distant
Belgian Congo. She had received only a week before a letter
from Toby—the first in over a year—which might have said the
following:


Barbara,

I am sorry that I once told you I loved you. I was
young and foolish and caught up in passion. Forgive me if that is possible. I am now married. I was

mustered out of the RAF after a near-fatal crash in the service of our beloved nation. I will survive but will always have to use a crutch because of a leg injury.

Remember the last gift I gave you? It was a new edition of the Bible which I found helpful in my struggles for sanity during this terrible conflict. I hope you will find some solace in reading from this same Holy Book. I do not know if we will ever meet again, but I will never forget you.

Sincerely,

Toby

This letter only deepened her sense of despair in the brutal isolation of her post, the insanity of the awful war, and the absence of any friend to whom she could pour out her heart and soul. She tried to keep calm and steady and take long walks alone on the beach when she was off duty. When she slept, she dreamed of Toby, of Aunt Elsie, of Seven Oaks, of trade school, of Cousin Harvey, and, above all, of being in a near-fatal crash.

Early one morning, she simply turned on the shortwave radio and sent this message to the post headquarters in Kirkwall: "I need to return home urgently. I can not take this assignment a day longer. My post mate, Fiona, can handle things until you send a replacement. Please, help. Lt. B. M. Mill."

The response from Captain Keller was immediate. He knew that she was near the breaking point and needed help right away. A military launch was dispatched to bring her back. Within a matter of hours, she was back in Kirkwall and put aboard an army supply plane heading south.

## At Craiglockhart Hospital in Edinburgh

An army nurse was assigned to accompany Barbara. They took a taxi from the military airport near Perth to Edinburgh. All the local cabbies knew the hospital and what it was for. On arrival at the hospital gate, Barbara, her mouth slightly open, stared up at the massive yellow grey facade of Craiglockhart.

"My God," she blurted.

Two khaki-wearing soldiers took her bags and walked up the marble staircase to the first floor.

"Here you are," they said.

Nurse Graham opened the door and stood aside as Barbara entered. "Come on in, the sooner we can see the admitting doctor, the better."

Dr. Rivers took a case sheet from the stack on his side table, paused a few moments to collect his thoughts, and might have penned the following report:

Patient Lt. Barbara Mary Mill joined the WAAF in November 1940, took training at Devon, and was assigned to an observer post in Sussex in April 1941. She was transferred to an isolated post on Papa Westray Island, Orkney Islands, in December 1943. Her service has been exemplary with no negative comments by her commanding officers.

Apparently, the patient suffered a nervous breakdown two weeks ago and was accompanied by an army nurse by boat and air to Craiglockhart Hospital, Edinburgh, today. The patient is suffering from signs of mental fatigue and finds it difficult to focus in the interview.

She was asked the following questions:

Q: Do you enjoy a good relationship with your family?
A: They are very far away. I haven't seen my parents for over four years. They are missionaries in the Belgian Congo. I have letters from them about every week. But I really haven't had the interest to write them for months.

Q: Do you have any mates to talk with and share some of your feelings?
A: Hell no. They just tell me to get over it.

Q: What is the "it" that you are referring to?
A: Oh, that's about Toby, who said he loved me and then betrayed me!

Q: How did he betray you?
A: The SOB got married and never told me there was somebody else. I just can't go on living like this! There is no one I can ever trust again!

With these words, Barbara broke into uncontrollable sobs, and a nurse was called in to give her a sedative.

After she had spent a few days in the hospital, her uncle and aunt who lived in Glasgow were contacted, and they came to see her. She had never really gotten to know them or their children, however, and Barbara said that the only real relatives she could talk to were the Starte cousins in Cambridge, where she had spent her adolescence.

Within a few weeks, the decision was made to move her to the Holburn Hospital near Cambridge so that she could be closer to her cousins. Her parents had been contacted, and they sent word that they were moving up their furlough dates and would be home from Africa by mid-1944.

Her parents returned to the shady lanes of Cambridge, leaving the dusty streets of Irema, Belgian Congo, behind. They settled in a small home at 10 Church Lane and tried to adjust to the pace of urban living, and Barbara was granted a weekend pass to visit her parents (see photo section following p. 82). Together, they attended the evensong at the local Anglican chapel, and Barbara felt comfortable in a simple, structured service rather than the large, more informal service at the St. Andrew Street Baptist Church.

Barbara's mother died a few years later, after which the visits with her father meant even more to both of them. They seemed to be at peace with each other.

She lived out her remaining years in the Holburn Hospital and died peacefully at the age of forty-six.

A simple service was held in the Cambridge Memorial Gardens, and her ashes were scattered on the same lawn where her mother's ashes were spread a decade before. Later, her father's ashes comingled with those of his wife and daughter. A pastor relative had the honor of pronouncing a final benediction over the earthly remains of the "Congo trio," long to be loved and honored.

# 17 | The Family Tree That Seemed to Wither

The Mill family originated in the Lowlands of Scotland, with roots for centuries in Clackmannanshire, and seldom emigrated abroad. Even though much of this heather seed did not scatter far, the impact of the lives of my mother, Clara Anna Mill, and her older brother, Alexander George Mill, left deep impressions on the lives of many. Uncle Alex and his faithful wife, Ethel, gave forty years of their lives to the people of the former Belgian Congo. Tens of thousands in the Baptist community of that great African nation remember Bamdombele and Mama Bamdombele (their African names) for their over thirty years of missionary service. My mother, married to a Scottish Baptist pastor, invested her life in rearing our family of six in Canada and the United States as a pastor's wife. She is lovingly remembered in the nine congregations they served over four decades.

In the twenty-first century, finding any roots and shoots of the Mill relatives is nearly impossible. Today, many Mills families exist, but very few Mill families can be found. Was the final *s* added to the names of families from the Mill lineage? While researching 1887 birth records (the year of my mother's birth), I discovered that thirty-four female babies in Glasgow were born that year with the family name "Mill." Thus over a century ago, there must have been a number of Mill families. Today, however, the telephone books in Edinburgh and Glasgow list only a handful of Mill names. Did the families leave Scotland? Did they have fewer male heirs to carry on the family name?

## Some Early Mill Progenitors

One line of ancestors goes back to Walter Mill, one of the first Protestant martyrs during the Scottish Reformation.

Another, more prolific, line leads to the family of the philosopher and economist John Stuart Mill (1806–1873). In *On Liberty* (1853), Mill eloquently defended individual freedom and, in *The Subjection of Women* (1869), made a strong yet controversial call for women's rights. My mother's nickname in school was "Millie the Philosopher," so the name "John Stuart Mill" must have still been in common parlance some decades later.

In the family story my mother wrote, *Transplanted Heather,* she relates that her grandfather Frederick Mill was a barber with a high-class clientele on Buchannon Street in Glasgow. She wrote, "He was genteel to a fault and liked to dress above his income. He spoke perfect English and yet always struggled to make ends meet. But he always kept up a good front!"

## Grandfather Frederick Stuart Mill (1860–1923)

In "Memories of My Father" (1948), my mother painted the following lovely vignette of her father:

> Your Grandfather Mill was gentle of spirit. In those days "the rod" was considered the best, if not the only way of successfully rearing children. But I can never recall my Father indulging in its use. He was handsome, six feet tall, slender, with dark eyes, coal black hair and a well formed nose.
>
> His mother died when he was two years old and he

was raised by a housekeeper. My father's start in life was precarious, so like Topsy he just "grew."

Father was free of pride. He was thoroughly democratic, hating all cant and hypocrisy. Nor was he endowed with leadership ability but he always built up our ego as children by encouraging us.

Early in their married life both had religious experiences which enriched their lives. . . . The Bible became a living book to us as children. Father also read widely in secular and religious history. Of worldly ambitions he had none. This was a cause of irritation between my business-like mother and him. Father's ambition was all in the realm of the spirit. He never saved a penny and his salary being very ordinary our mother found it hard to be satisfied with her frustrated ambition for our standard of living. But we always paid our debts!

Father liked to sing. After we were bedded he would enter the room and say, "Now children, let us solemnize our thoughts." He would lead us in singing his favorite verse of "Loved with Everlasting Love":

> Heaven above is softer blue,
> Earth around is sweeter green,
> Christless eyes have never seen,
> Birds with gladder songs o'er flow,
> Earth with deeper beauties shine,
> Since I know as I am known'
> I am His and He is mine.

## Three Mill Cousins We Remember Well

They were born and reared in the middle-class suburb of
Bearsden, Glasgow, in the early 1900s. Father Gladstone was
employed in a financial office in downtown Glasgow. Mother
Jean seemed content in her role as wife and mother of three
boys and a girl. Sadness engulfed the family in 1918 when one
of the twin boys, "wee Archie," was taken in a typhoid epidemic. His surviving twin, Gladdie, married a delightful Irish
girl, Mae, and together they owned a small deli. The daughter, Marian, known as "Mari," worked as a court stenographer
and married Willie Beverage, a news reporter for the *Glasgow
Herald* who had the distinction of covering the Nuremberg
Trials and wrote many articles on the Celtic origins of Scottish words and customs.

Freddie, the eldest son, was the cousin our family came
to know well. He was definitely the favorite of his six American Sinclairs. Most of us had the joy of receiving the warm
hospitality he and his wife, Dorie, showered upon us when visiting their home in Glasgow. He worked in a financial office in
downtown Glasgow for many years. His poor eyesight caused
him to be assigned to home duty with the Royal Air Force
during World War II. Casualties were high in the RAF, so he
lost many of his friends. His yearning for peace is clearly felt
in this poem he wrote after the war:

### Village War Memorial

Above the brae stands a lone granite cross,
    a sad reminder of our two wars lost.
As I read them, my mind goes back: there was Jock,

the porter, grand old lad,

There was Dominic, the doctor, and blacksmith Sam.

Who alas at school I remember them well,

what in the divers can anyone tell,

That their lives would be cut short in

a carnage of hell.

Brave souls all who answered the call,

to end war's horrors only to fall.

Their sacrifice at last was to be in vain,

when a new generation had to fight again

And as once more the names I scan,

I think of man's injustice to man;

While the tears roll down my now aged face,

I remember still those who died in my place.

So before its too late, let's shout

"Ban nuclear arms for ever more."

Even though he and Dorie never had children of their own, he is remembered for his great love of children. The following poem revealed this passion in his life:

### By Candlelight

Tis strange but true that when in bed with candle lit

quite near my head,

I see, beside me on the wall, the oddest folk who

come to call.

And I lie without a sound, the pictures move and
    dance around,
And though it's hard to make them out, I know
    them all without a doubt.
There's Bo Peep looking for her sheep, Miss Muffet,
    too, about to weep,
And yes, there's Jack along with Jill, about to tumble
    down the hill.
Then as I watch I hear a sound; it's Wee Willie
    Winkie coming around,
And when I nod my sleepy head, I hear "Good
    Night" all around my bed.

He also enjoyed watercolor and oil painting. Through his brother and sister, our family inherited two of his paintings: a watercolor of the Iona Abbey (the cradle of Scottish religious faith) and an oil painting of Loch-an-Eilean Castle (see photo section following p. 82).

    Freddie was always respectful of the religious convictions and vocations of his American cousins, but religion was not on his radar. He was a secular Scot, as was his wife. Mother would say, "They never darkened a church door." We know that at Dorie's burial service, there was no officiating clergy and only a memorial tribute presented by a family member, Willie MacCreadie. We commend these beloved cousins to the eternal keeping of their Merciful and Loving Creator.

**Two Sons Carry on the Family Name**

As a tribute to our beloved Uncle Alex, my wife and I chose to enshrine his memory in the middle names of two of our three sons: David Mill Sinclair (b. 1947) and Paul Alexander Sinclair (b. 1953). Both of them have lived up to their great-uncle's goal to love one's neighbor as oneself and have chosen the field of social work, working with vulnerable members of society.

# 18 | A Chilean Graduate Student Connects with His Scottish Roots

Gabriel Raúl Sinclair Rodriguez had done very well at St. Andrew's College in Valparaíso when he graduated. He was rather fluent in English since his family conversed easily in both Spanish and English. In fact, he was born in the United States while his parents were doing their graduate work. His interests were definitely in the social sciences and, of course, in soccer and basketball.

He was interested in talking with his parents about his bicultural background. He was born in the United States and could travel with both Chilean and American passports. Questions like these came up in family conversations:

"Mother, where will I live when I finish college—Chile or the United States?"

"Dad, when will I ever get to know some of my American cousins, aunts, and uncles?"

"Will I ever get to travel to Scotland and see some of the places you visited when you were a boy?"

His mother, Marcela, brought up the subject as she and his father, Mark, strolled one day along the beach: "Mi querido, I have been thinking that perhaps our dear son might have an opportunity during his university studies in Chile to spend a year in the country of your father's ancestors and learn some of the fascinating history of the Scots. I think that at twenty-one he is mature enough to travel there on his own."

Mark responded quickly, "Why I have been thinking much the same, but I wasn't sure how you felt about his being away for a whole year. And there is an outside chance that he might have the chance of winning a *bolsa* to make that possible."

They continued to walk along as they looked out on the vast sweep of ocean that covered the horizon—beyond lay New Zealand and Australia some six thousands miles away.

"But what are the chances that he might have the good fortune to get a *bolsa?*" asked Marcela. "The competition is fierce since so many students at St. Andrew's want to study abroad."

"Let's talk to him first about it to see what he thinks," replied Mark. "Then if he seems interested, the next step would be to check with Principal Gutiérrez to see if he knows of any scholarship possibilities."

For many years the former British Empire had several institutions that focused on preparing foreign nationals for employment in the British Overseas Service. They had high standards, and getting a scholarship was tough going. Most of those institutions had disappeared, but the British Council was one such agency that had survived. It continued largely because of the conditions of the will of Lord Hammerfield, who gave the council the largest part of its endowment. He had written into his will that "the scholarship assistance provided in perpetuity by the Council should not depend only on the needs of the overseas service of the Crown, but prepare overseas students to nurture the British culture and language throughout the entire world."

Principal Gutiérrez readily found the address of the British Council in Oxford. Soon the application papers were ready for Gabriel. One of the questions that he had to answer carefully was, "Why do you wish to study British history as a part of your professional preparation?"

After some long discussions around the dining room table with his sister and parents, he came up with this statement:

I am Gabriel Raúl Sinclair Rodriquez. I graduated with honors from St. Andrew's College in Valparaíso, Chile. I plan to become a history teacher and specialize in British history. Because of the historic relationships between Great Britain and Chile since the time of our national independence to today, I feel that this subject will be even more important in the future with changes in the world economy.

I have a personal reason for wanting to study British history. I think my great-great-great-grandfather on my mother's side might have been James Collie Sinclair, a Scottish mercenary soldier in the Sinclair-Gunn Regiment of the British Legion, which fought with our patriots to win Chilean independence from Spain in the 1810s. He married a Chilean woman who was probably María Balfour de Aguilar of Valparaíso. On my father's side of the family, the Sinclairs have roots in the United States, Canada, and Scotland that have been traced back to 1066 when our family progenitor, Sir William Sinclair, came over from Normandy and fought with William the Conqueror at the Battle of Hastings.

I want to study at the University of Edinburgh to explore the early commercial, social, and political connections between the Scottish people and the Chilean nation. Since the archives of that period of Scottish history are located in Scotland, I believe that I can best accomplish my goal by doing a doctoral research program there.

And so it was.

Since nearly all the remaining Sinclair connections in Scotland were by then only family history, young Gabriel flew off to Great Britain with the address of a third cousin of his grandfather and the telephone number of a friend of a cousin of his great-grandmother Clara Anna Sinclair. Grandpa John promised to write a letter of introduction so that Gabriel would have some distant relatives in Edinburgh to contact. He was a lad with sufficient self-confidence, and his parents really didn't worry. He liked people, and people were attracted to his easy, laid-back ways.

Since the dorm room he was supposed to share with a student from Ghana was unavailable the week before orientation, he was assigned to stay at the university guesthouse just off High Street. As he signed the guest register, his curiosity had him leafing through a few pages to see what names appeared in recent years. He paged back to 2008, 2006, 2000, and then to his amazement, his eyes fixed on the name "Sinclair." His next glance caught the full name of a guest in May 2000: "John Henderson Sinclair."

"That's my grandfather, who was here eighteen years ago!" he thought to himself.

Then he remembered a conversation with his dad in

Chile about the many trips the Sinclair family had made to Scotland in the 1940s and 1950s and the trip his own father took in 1969 when he was twelve.

"I can't believe I'm staying in the same guesthouse my grandfather John stayed in eighteen years ago. Even though I miss my family and friends back in Chile, I feel more at home."

As Gabriel settled into his studies, he often sought assistance in the university library from an attractive young woman who was a student research assistant. He knew only that her name was Margaret Nicolson.

On one occasion, as he was working through the records of Castle Sinclair-Girnigoe near Wick, Margaret noticed the name "Gabriel Raúl Sinclair Rodriguez" on his library card. She looked rather surprised that this Chilean graduate student would have "Sinclair" as his middle name. She knew that her great-great-grandmother was a Sinclair married to a Nicolson.

And so their conversation developed into an invitation to share a cup of tea together in the college cafeteria and talk about their family histories.

"I just can't believe that you have Caithness roots back to the eighteenth and nineteenth centuries!" Margaret exclaimed. "I know that Granny Maggie once said the name 'Margaret' had been in the Nicolson family for several generations. When I'm back in Thurso on holiday, I'll check in the county genealogical records to see what turns up. Did you say that you think that your great-great-grandfather's son James fought in Chile in the 1810s for the freedom of your country from Spain?"

Gabriel was certain that his father and mother had often told him that some of his forebears on his mother's side came from Scotland during the time of the "Liberator," Bernardo O'Higgins. He promised himself to ask them the next time they talked on the phone.

After several weeks and a few more tea breaks together at the U's cafeteria, Gabriel invited Margaret to be his guest at a university history club program. After the event he walked her back to her apartment on Mackay Street, which she shared with a couple of students who also worked at the university library. She said that she had told her parents about meeting him and that he had Caithness connections through his ancestors in Chile. Her parents said that they would be glad to put him in touch with a local genealogist if he ever came as far north in Scotland as Thurso. They also said that they would be glad for him to stay at their home since their children were now grown or away at school. The invitation sounded like genuine Scottish hospitality.

This seemed to be an opening for Gabriel to take a step further in their friendship. He didn't think that he was falling in love with Margaret, but he did like to be with her and enjoyed her pleasant, nonchalant manners. She was serious but not too much so.

She would make a stab at speaking to him in pidgin Spanish, saying, "Cómo está, señor? Te gusta éste clima tan mala de Scotland?"

Gabriel would respond, "No comprendo. No speaka dah Spanish!"

Margaret and Gabriel bought bus tickets from Edinburgh to Thurso when the term vacation began in mid-April—just ten days. The twelve-hour bus trip for him was like traveling south from Santiago to Puerto Montt—a journey that took him by lakes and rivers and through green valleys surrounded by hills and, in the far distance, a range of rather high mountains.

He thought, "These scenes remind me of southern Chile when we traveled to vacation at my great-uncle's farm."

The Nicolson home was modest but large enough to have a guest room. A fire burned in the stone fireplace, which took the chill off the early winter in the northern Highlands.

"Welcome to our home, Gabriel," said Margaret's father. "We have heard of your Caithness roots from Margaret. We hope you won't be disappointed with the Nicolsons and our neighbors. We're just ordinary Scots, but all of us are aware of much of our family history and, may I say, humbly proud of it."

Gabriel and Margaret walked down to the Thurso wharf and watched the ferries to the Orkneys come and go. The islands were just two hours away by ferry. She told him that many Orkadians were related to the northern Scots and that many families had immigrated to Canada and other parts of the British Empire. They searched for Sinclair and Nicolson tombstones in an old cemetery and found a few, but the graves were not too well cared for, thought Gabriel.

At dinner one evening, her father asked what he knew about the Sinclairs and Nicolsons. He vaguely remembered his father's mentioning his forebears were originally tenant farmers from around Halkirk and that his great-great-great-grandfather William Sinclair was a kind of carpenter who made wooden parts for farm implements, like plows, sickles, and wagons.

"That's interesting," replied Margaret's father. "I remember Granny Maggie telling me about her great-grandmother

Margaret Nicolson, who apparently 'married below her class.' So her husband was probably not too well educated or was some kind of artisan. His last name was 'Henderson.'"

"Henderson?" Gabriel stopped. "Why that's been a family name among the Sinclairs for nine generations. It's in my cousin's long name, which includes his father's name, my grandfather's middle name, and our family name. Listen to it: 'Ian Paul Henderson Sinclair.' Impressive, huh?"

The vacation days sped by as Margaret and Gabriel did a lot of things together. Every passing day, they found that they had more in common than just Caithness roots. Gabriel couldn't call his feelings love yet, but it was certainly more than mutual admiration. Their friendship kindled Margaret's interest in studying another field. She liked her work at the library, but perhaps she, too, could become a history teacher. She certainly knew a great deal about research methodology. Back in Edinburgh after the long vacation, they saw more and more of each other.

"Gabriel, don't be surprised," Margaret said. "I have decided to go back to the university and get a second degree. This time it will be in Pacific Rim history. This new branch of contemporary history has been sparked by the great interest in the economy, politics, and culture of the rim of the Pacific Ocean. Asian countries, especially China, Japan, and Korea, are making considerable investments in countries on the Pacific coast of South America—nations like Colombia, Ecuador, Peru, and Chile. The Koreans are planning a new rail system between Argentina and Chile in order to have access to the Atlantic side of South America."

"That's a great idea, Margaret," Gabriel responded. "A great deal of study is being projected on this subject for the coming decades. Perhaps after you do the coursework here in Scotland, you could get a British Council scholarship and do your research in Chile."

Margaret had definitely been taken by the possibility that she and Gabriel might have more than a common career and build a life together. Marriage, perhaps? But could she ever leave her family and friends in Scotland and live so far away? Would Gabriel ever consider settling in Great Britain? Could he establish a teaching career here? Many foreign-born teachers wanted to teach in Great Britain, and competition was fierce.

Years later, the following entry appeared in a bibliography published by UNESCO under "Development Studies Related to the Pacific Rim and South American Economics, 2015–2023":

Pai Ramos, Minsoo. *Korean Economic Colonies in South America, 1975–2020.*

Sinclair-Rodriguez, Gabriel Raúl, and Margaret Nicolson de Sinclair. *Chilean Economic Development and Economic Ties with Australia and New Zealand, 1993–2023.* Santiago, Chile: Austral Publications, 2024.

# Epilogue

Alex Sinclair Mitchell and Natalia Alondra Sinclair-Rodriguez met by chance as both were making stenciled copies of faded inscriptions on Sinclair graves in an old cemetery, called El Cementerio de Disidentes, overlooking the Bay of Valparaíso (see photo section following p. 82). Alex was a twenty-three-year-old graduate student in history from Cape Town, South Africa. Natalia was an eighteen-year-old university student from Con Con, Chile.

"Cómo está, señorita?" said Alex, introducing himself. "Me llamo, Alejandro. Vengo de Africa del sur para estudiar la historia militar de Chile. Tengo un interes en particular de los archivos y reliquias de la Legion Britanica de los tiempos del General San Martin."

"My name is Natalia Sinclair-Rodriguez. I know English since my father is an American. I spent nine years of my childhood in Minnesota," Natalia replied.

"That's great," said Alex somewhat relieved. "I really don't speak Spanish very well. I went to the city hall, and they told me that this land—about two acres—was purchased by a British colony in 1832 for their dead since the Roman Catholic bishop wouldn't let Protestants be buried in the city cemetery. They also told me that some of the remains of the early burials during the war for Chilean independence were removed from the military cemetery and reburied here. I understand that, here in Chile in those days, all non-Catholics were called *disidentes*.

"Did you say that your family name is Sinclair? Why that's

my middle name. My full name is Alexander Sinclair Mitchell. My great-great-grandfather was a Sinclair from Inverness,
Scotland. In fact, I'm actually trying to research the Sinclairs
who were here fighting for Chilean independence at the time
of San Martin in the early nineteenth century. What a coinci-
dence to meet you here! I can hardly believe it."

"Neither can I," Natalia responded. "My grandfather visited South Africa in 2000 and met some descendents of the first
Sinclairs to settle there. I have a term paper due next month
about the foreign mercenaries who fought with General San
Martin for our independence. Perhaps we can help each other
with our research."

"Sure," smiled Alex. "Let's get together soon. I have to
run to meet a friend right now. Would you give me your cell
number? I'll call you tomorrow. I'm thrilled to know more
about your Sinclair connection with Chile."

The seeds of the heather continue to drop, and the Sinclair saga goes on!

## Appendix A
## The Ancestral Site of the Sinclairs of Calder

The farm is known as Achavarigil and is located in the Calder neighborhood three miles west of the village of Halkirk in Caithness, Scotland. The name is shown on the modern utility pole at the entrance to the property. The earliest known record of the name and location is an ordinance map dated 1803. Two of the tenant families were the William Millers and the William Sinclairs. The Sinclair plot was 1.1 acres. Their neighbors were the James Macbeaths with a 5.3-acre plot. The author has a copy of the old map. Mr. Macbeath signed as witness to the birth of the first children of William and Barbara Sinclair. This stone croft house may have been the original building but is now used as a storage barn (see photo section following p. 82).

## Appendix B
## Genealogy of John Henderson Sinclair
## Seven Generations since 1761

1. William Sinclair (1761–1840) and Barbara Harrow (1772–1835)

2. Henderson Sinclair (1815–1890) and Margaret Nicolson (1820–1890)

3. Henderson Sinclair (1857–1935) and Martha Jane Peat (1857–1923)

4. John Peat Sinclair (1887–1955) and Clara Anna Mill (1887–1977)

5. John Henderson Sinclair (1924–) and Lillian Maxine Banta (1919–)

6. John Mark Sinclair (1957–) and Marcela Jasmin Rodriguez Aquilar (1965–)

7. Natalia Alondra Sinclair Rodriquez (1992–)

Gabriel Raul Sinclair Rodriquez (1997–)

## Appendix C
## Families and Countries Referred to in the Narrative

1. Immigration to the Americas
Chapter 2: Stobo–Park family
Chapter 3: James Collie Sinclair descendents in Chile★
Chapter 18: Sinclair–Aguilar family in Chile★

2. Immigration to Canada
Chapter 8: William Sinclair and Isabella Jack descendents in Canada
Chapter 10: Henderson "Harry" Sinclair family in Canada
Chapter 11: Descendents of Robert Peat Sinclair in the United States★
Chapter 14: Family of John Peat Sinclair and Clara Anna Mill in the United States
Chapter 15: Children of Clara Mill Sinclair and Baxter Carlise Hurn in the United States

3. Immigration to South Africa
Chapter 4: Descendents of Kennett Sinclair and Susanna Dell

4. Immigration to Punjab, Pakistan
Chapter 7: Descendents of Margaret Henderson and Amir Massurif★

5. Immigration to Australia and New Zealand
Chapter 6: Descendents of George Sinclair and Patricia Anderson★

6. Immigration to the United States

Chapter 8: Descendents of Daniel Boone Sinclair★

Chapter 12: Descendents of George Struan Robertson★

★Indicates a lack of documentation

# Notes

Preface

1. Andrew Sinclair, *Blood and Kin: An Empire Saga* (London: Sinclair-Stevenson, 2002).

Prologue

1. James T. Calder, *History of Caithness: Sketch of the Civil and Traditional History of Caithness for the Twentieth Century* (Wick, Scotland: n.p., 1887).

Chapter 2

1. "The Design of Darien," *Journal of Presbyterian History* 17, no. 1:14.

2. Ibid., 34.

3. Ibid., 12.

4. *The Pictorial History of Scotland,* vol. 1 (London: Virtue and Co., n.d.), 525.

5. James Walker, *John Knox and His Ideas and Ideals* (London: A. C. Armstrong and Son, 1905), 5

6. "The Design of Darien," 84.

7. Theodore Roosevelt to Rev. Henry McCook, Presbyterian Historical Society, rare documents, R677t(2).

Chapter 3

1. Humberto Lagos Schuffeneger and Arturo Chacon Herrera, *La Religion en las Fuerzas Armadas y de Orden* (Santiago, Chile: Lar y Presor, 1987), 21–23.

## Chapter 5

1. Hans P. Rheinheimer, *TOPO: The Story of a Scottish Colony Near Caracas, 1825–27* (Edinburgh: Scottish Academic Press, 1988).

2. Ibid.

3. Guelph Historical Society, *Historic Guelph: The Royal City* (Guelph, Ontario: Guelph Historical Society, 1976).

## Chapter 6

1. Thomas Keneally, *The Great Shame and the Triumph of the Irish in the English-Speaking World* (New York: Doubleday, 1998), 46.

## Chapter 8

1. Federal Writers' Project, "American Life Stories, 1936–1940," oral interview, ms (Washington, D.C.: Library of Congress).

## Chapter 9

1. Land records, Manitoba Immigration Office, official text of land survey document of Township No. 11, Range XXII—West, 1881.

## Chapter 10

1. Military records of Canadian Expeditionary Force, British War Memorial, Edinburgh, Scotland.

## Chapter 11

1. Census records of Scotland, 1905.

Chapter 15

1. Clare (Hurn) Sinclair, *As Way Opens: My Life* (Privately printed, 2000), 438.

Chapter 16

1. Letter, 5 May 1924, correspondence of Alexander G. Mill and Ethel Starte Mill, collection of the Baptist Missionary Society of Great Britain, Angus Library, Oxford University.

2. Letter, 4 July 1928.

3. Letter, 11 July 1929.

4. Letter, 21 March 1944.

5. Ibid.

6. Letter, 10 June 1944.

7. Letter, 15 July 1944.

# Bibliography

Anderson, Mark R. D. *Familiae Morganiae et Dunbar Andersones: The History of the Anderson, Morgan, Spoor, Holmes, Sinclair, Cawood, Dunbar, and Wedder Burn Families.* 2nd ed. Cape Town, South Africa: privately printed, 2003 (PO Box 12, Constantia Cape, 7848 South Africa).

Calder, James T. *History of Caithness: Sketch of the Civil and Traditional History of Caithness for the Twentieth Century.* Wick, Scotland, 1887.

Hersey, John. *The Call.* New York: Alfred A. Knopf, 1985.

Gittings, James A. *Bread, Meat, and Raisins after the Dance.* Palos Verdes, CA: Morgan Press, 1997.

Guelph Historical Society. *Historic Guelph: The Royal City.* Guelph, Ontario: Guelph Historical Society, 1976.

Keneally, Thomas. *The Great Shame and the Triumph of the Irish in the English-Speaking World.* New York: Doubleday, 1998.

Ludwig, Emil. *Napoleon.* Translated by Eden and Cedar Paul. London: Arden Library, 1926.

Mackay, John. *The Church in Highlands, or the Progress of Evangelical Religion in Gaelic Scotland, 1563–1843.* New York: Hodder and Stroughton, 1914.

Morrison, Leonard Allison. *The History of the Sinclair Family in Europe and America for Eleven Hundred Years.* Boston: Damrell and Upham, 1896.

Peebles, John. *The Highland Clearances.* New York: Penguin Books, 1993.

*The Pictorial History of Scotland.* Vol. 1. London: Virtue and Co., n.d.

Rheinheimer, Hans P. *TOPO: The Story of a Scottish Colony Near Caracas, 1825–27.* Edinburgh: Scottish Academic Press, 1988.

Saint Clair, L. A. de, *Historie Genealogique de la Familiae de Saint Clair et de Ses Alianices Franco-Ecosse.* Paris: Imprimiere Hardy and Bernard, 1909.

*The Scottish Clans and Their Tartans.* 32nd ed. Edinburgh: W. and A. K. Johnston, 1946.

Sinclair, Andrew. *Blood and Kin: An Empire Saga.* London: Sinclair-Stevenson, 2002.

Sinclair, Clara Anna (Mill). "Transplanted Heather." Unpublished manuscript, 1949.

———. "Memories of My Father." Unpublished manuscript, 1950.

Sinclair, Clare (Hurn). *As Way Opens: My Life.* Privately printed, 2000.

Sinclair, John Henderson. *In All Faith and Tenderness.* Roseville, MN: privately printed, 2003.

———. "The Life of Bandombele and Mama Bandombele of the Congo." Unpublished manuscript, 1991.

———. *My Life Story.* Roseville, MN: privately printed, 2006.

Sinclair, Maxine Banta. *Maxine's Memoirs.* Roseville, MN: privately printed, 2002.

Stokes, Margaret. *Descendents of George Sinclair, 1739–2000: A Study of Nine Generations.* Melbourne, Australia: privately printed, 2000.

Walker, James. *John Knox and His Ideas and Ideals.* London: A. C. Armstrong and Son, 1905.